MURDER IS A NIGHTMARE

A HANNAH KLINE MYSTERY

PAULA BERNSTEIN

M&Z PRESS

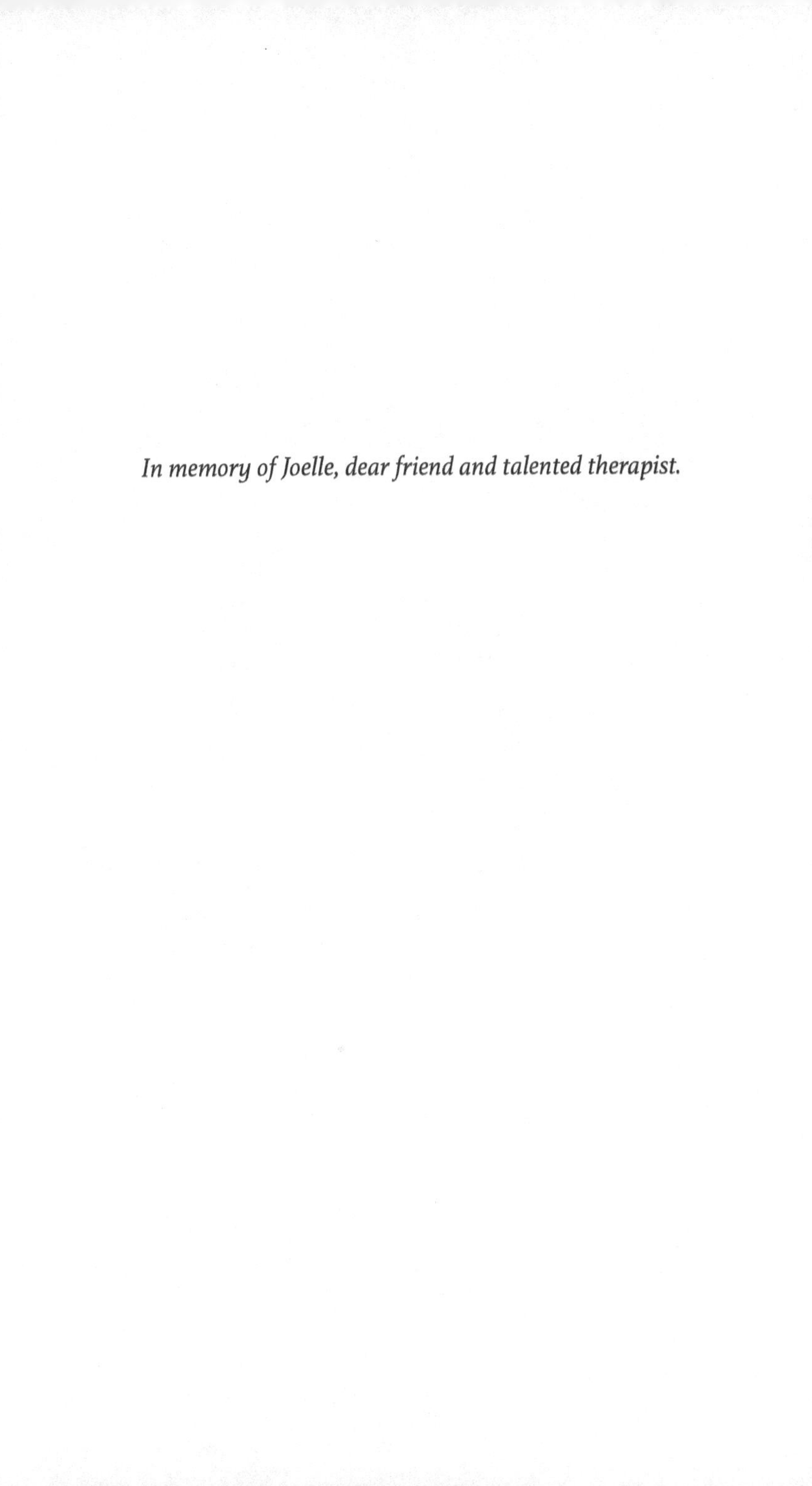

In memory of Joelle, dear friend and talented therapist.

PROLOGUE
DECEMBER 2014

Dr. Andrea Marcus finished her workout, flushed, sweaty and satisfied. She'd needed the exercise. It helped to deal with the increasing stress of her practice. Everything had been fine until she accepted a new psychiatric patient into her Friday noon slot. For the past several weeks her anxiety and fear had been escalating. Thankfully, her office was closed until after the New Year, so she didn't have to think about him.

In the plush locker room, she retrieved her gym bag, took a warm shower, sprayed her body with a jasmine-scented cologne, and applied lotion to her arms and legs. She dressed in jeans and a new white T shirt, tied her sneakers, and brushed out her long hair. She had made brunch reservations for herself, and her husband Jonathan, at their favorite Malibu restaurant. Afterward, they were planning on a romantic afternoon at home, before picking up their daughter Molly from her play date. She took a last look in the mirror. She was ready for brunch and for an afternoon of great sex. Humming to herself, she retrieved her car keys and headed out to the parking lot.

There were fewer cars at this hour on a Sunday morning, but some jerk with a huge minivan had parked right next to her. She hated minivans. Even when they parked between the lines, they took up so much space she could never open her car door all the way. It was a good thing she was thin.

Heading first to the passenger side door, she opened it, and tossed her gym bag and jacket onto the seat. She slammed the door shut and walked around to the driver's side. As she reached for the handle, a muscular arm pulled her backwards and a gloved hand covered her mouth.

Remembering her self-defense classes, she began to bend forward and kick. Before she could swing her leg, she felt a sharp, painful stab in her upper arm. Her head began to spin, her legs felt weak. The man pulled her arms behind her, and she felt the cold metal of a pair of handcuffs immobilizing her hands. She screamed, but her shout came out as a croak.

The man picked her up, hefted her over his shoulder and carried her to the back of the minivan. As he laid her down, she caught a glimpse of a beard. She was feeling dizzy and disoriented; her vision began to blur. The man covered her with a blanket. She tried to say something, but before the sound emerged, the world went dark.

BOOK 1

OCTOBER 2014

CHAPTER ONE

Psychiatrist Andrea Marcus hadn't wanted to accept a new patient. She resented having to give up her lunch hour. Three years ago, when Molly was born, she promised herself to limit her practice to thirty hours a week. This new patient, Blake Harris, brought her census up to thirty-one.

When she opened the door to her waiting room, she found him seated on the straight-backed chair she'd installed for her elderly patients. He appeared to be in his mid-thirties, clean cut, with short sandy hair, wearing a tan polo shirt and khakis. His knees were tightly pressed together and his hands were clasped on his lap. He gazed at her through round, wire-rimmed glasses, his thin lips without expression.

"I'm Dr. Marcus. Please come in, Mr. Harris." Andrea motioned toward the door of her consult room.

"It's Dr. Harris," he said, as he followed her in.

He seated himself on her sofa, as far away from her armchair as he could get.

"Are you a physician?" Andrea asked. He reminded her

of one of those math nerds in high school who always sat alone at lunchtime.

"PhD."

"In?"

"Cancer Biology."

Andrea leaned forward. "Your internist told me that you needed to be seen immediately. How can I help you?"

"I don't know if you can, but he insisted I see a shrink. He's tried everything else. I've been having nightmares for weeks and they're interfering with my functioning. I can't afford to be at less than my best."

He removed his glasses, yawned and rubbed his eyes. Andrea could see there were dark circles underneath them.

"I'm the founder of a start-up company. We've been very successful and are in the process of negotiating a buy-out for a considerable sum."

"I can see why you'd want to be at the top of your game," Andrea said. "These nightmares you've been having. Are they all different? Or the same dream?"

"They're variations on a theme. I've tried sleeping pills and anti-anxiety drugs. None of them seem to work. In fact, they make things worse. It's harder to end the nightmare by waking up when I'm drugged. Once I'm awake, no matter what I do, I can't go back to sleep."

"Can you describe the theme?"

"I don't remember all of my dreams in detail, but they all involve water. Last night, I dreamt I was driving over a bridge. I lost control of my car and landed in the river. The water started to come in and I couldn't get the door open to swim to the surface. I knew I was going to drown, and then I woke up."

"Tell me more."

"What difference does it make?"

"It may help me figure out what's triggering them.

There's a great deal science doesn't understand about sleep. I like to think of dreams as messages from your unconscious mind. If a nightmare is recurring, it suggests that there is something your subconscious wants your conscious mind to remember. Once it does, there may be no need for the dreams to continue."

There was a long silence.

Andrea waited it out.

Finally, he looked up at her. "I was alone, driving a sports car, very fast. There was a sense of urgency, as if there was something I had to do. I needed to cross the bridge."

"Sometimes, in dreams," Andrea said, "a bridge represents a transition from one aspect of your life to another. For example, from being single to getting married, or moving away from home to a new place. You mentioned that you were in the midst of a major negotiation involving your company. Is that a transition that might be causing you a sense of urgency or a fear of drowning?"

"I hadn't thought of that. Are you suggesting that the thought of my company being taken over by a bigger one makes me feel as if I'm going to drown?"

Andrea waited while he thought about it. She often found that silence produced interesting insights.

"I have some mixed feelings about selling out. I'd make a fortune but I'd lose control of my company. Maybe I need to rethink it."

"How long have these nightmares been happening?" she asked.

"Six weeks. Maybe seven."

"Can you think of anything that happened in your life, six or seven weeks ago, that might have triggered the first one? Perhaps if you reviewed your calendar and emails during that period, it might refresh your memory."

Blake removed his phone from its belt clip and brought up the calendar app. He scrolled back six weeks.

"I've found something. I don't know if it's relevant. Family dinner, the first one in a long time."

"Can you tell me about your family and your childhood?"

"That's a tall order, Doc. Where to start...what do you want to know?"

"Whatever you'd like me to know."

"I grew up in Newport Beach. Dad was in financial services. He invested other people's money and made a bundle doing it. Mother spent her time spending his money and hanging out with other rich wives who liked shopping and going out to lunch. I have a brother who's eight years older. I was an accident. My brother referred to me as the hole in the condom."

Andrea restrained a laugh and continued to look at him with an attentive expression, waiting for him to continue.

"My parents shouldn't have had kids. The only time my father spent with me was when he wanted to tell me how to live my life. He was a little controlling. My mother was happiest when she could leave me with the nanny and take off with her friends. She had no idea of how to interact with either of us."

"It sounds as if you had a difficult childhood." Andrea glanced at her watch. "I'm afraid we're almost out of time. For our next session, try to remember everything you can about that dinner. Perhaps we'll be able to identify the trigger for your dreams. I'd also like you to keep a pad of paper and a pen on your bedside table, and whenever you have a nightmare, write down all the details and bring the information with you."

"What makes you so sure I'm coming back?"

"You strike me as a guy who isn't a quitter. You're also a

scientist, so you know the value of data. I need more data if you want my help solving your problem."

His eyebrows rose and he stood up, reached into his back pocket for a wallet, and removed a check. "I don't believe I remembered to ask your fee when I made the appointment. What do I owe you?"

"I charge three-hundred and fifty dollars for a session," Andrea said.

"Really? Are you sure you're worth three-fifty?"

"That is my fee. It will be up to you to decide if it's worth it to you."

Blake Harris walked over to her desk, helped himself to a pen, and wrote the check. "Here's a payment for the first month. Then, just like any new hire in my company, I'll evaluate your productivity and decide if you're worth keeping."

He placed the check on her desk.

"Same time, next week," he said.

And he walked out of her office without a backward glance.

Andrea blew out a breath, clenched her fists, and looked at her watch. She had twenty minutes to finish off her yogurt and apple before the next patient. Her stomach was churning the way it had just before her medical boards. She didn't need a disrespectful, hostile, controlling new patient. She opened the vanilla yogurt, took a spoonful, and spilled it onto the jacket of her designer suit. Cursing under her breath, she returned to the utility room, wet a paper towel, and dabbed at the mess. The next time Dr. Harris came in for a session, she was going to wear something less expensive to clean.

CHAPTER TWO

BLAKE HARRIS EXITED THE MEDICAL BUILDING onto Wilshire Boulevard in Westwood Village. He hadn't bothered to take his car. His apartment was within walking distance, and he hated giving his new hundred thousand dollar Maserati to a valet. At least at home and at the office, it was in a secure garage with a reserved parking spot.

His stomach signaled that he would do well to grab some lunch before returning to work, so he walked over to Tender Greens and ordered the Happy Vegan Salad. He prided himself on his thin, muscular body, and the combination of daily workouts with his private trainer, and his recent dietary discipline, was keeping him in optimum shape.

As he sipped his iced herbal tea, he entered next week's psychiatry appointment into his phone's calendar. He had doubted Andrea Marcus would be of much help, despite his internist's insistence that she was brilliant and insightful, but he had to admit, her suggestion about the upcoming business negotiation had gotten him thinking about whether he really wanted the sale to go through.

One thing his internist had failed to mention was that Andrea was hot. He smiled, visualizing the beautiful face with the high cheekbones, brilliant blue eyes and clear lip gloss, framed by a curtain of long, honey-colored hair. She was almost as tall as he was, and her designer pantsuit did little to conceal the voluptuous body underneath. It was worth the hourly fee just to sit opposite her.

CHAPTER THREE

A NDREA COULDN'T WAIT FOR HER LAST PATIENT to be finished so she could leave the office and go home. It wasn't like her to find herself so annoyed after a psychotherapy session. She knew better. She shouldn't be reacting to his provocation. She should be analyzing it and using it as a tool to understand him.

Home was a ten minute drive to the east side of Westwood Village, where the charming old houses and large trees could make her forget she lived a stone's throw from bustling Wilshire Boulevard. Pulling into the garage of her 1920s Spanish Revival home, she opened the door to the kitchen.

"Mommy, look what I drew at nursery school." Molly was at the kitchen table with milk and cookies, and Carla was cutting up salad vegetables.

Andrea put down her purse and lifted her chubby, blonde, three-year-old into her arms. "Show me."

Molly wiggled out of her arms and presented her with an elaborate set of drawings.

"These are terrific," Andrea said. "Is that supposed to be you and me and Daddy?"

"Yes, and there's our kitty." The kitty took up about half the space.

"We don't have a kitty," Andrea said.

"But we have to get one. Zoe has two." Zoe was the six-year-old daughter of Andrea's closest friend and fellow physician, Hannah Kline.

"Well, we'll talk to Daddy about it later. Mommy's going to change into some comfy clothes."

After dinner and Molly's bedtime, Andrea took a mug of tea into the den so she could vent to her husband, Jonathan. The two of them had met six years ago, when Andrea was a senior resident assigned to the Oncology Consultation service, and Jonathan was an Oncology fellow. The attraction had been instant, and still was, even after five years of marriage. As she looked at his tall, slim body, his handsome, craggy face with its deep brown eyes and and gentle mouth, she felt a flush of desire. He smiled at her and made room on the sofa, focusing on her face and listening to her with complete attention. She'd always thought men who knew how to listen were particularly sexy.

"I got this exasperating new patient today. He acted as if I were interviewing for a job in his mailroom. It's been quite a while since I've met anyone quite so annoying."

"Tell him you're not a good fit for him, and refer him out."

"I'd love to, but the internist who sent him is a valued colleague. I need to try to treat him despite the fact that he seems narcissistic and controlling. He's obviously getting off on trying to demonstrate that he's smarter than I am."

Jonathan was seated at the other end of the sofa. He moved closer and began massaging her feet. "I know you can't name names, but do you know anything about him that might be helpful in formulating a therapeutic approach?"

Andrea shrugged and wiggled her toes. She was a sucker for a foot massage. She was also feeling a little guilty complaining to him. He worked so hard. Ordinarily, she'd have phoned Hannah, but Hannah was on her honeymoon. The last thing she needed was a phone call from Andrea whining about an obnoxious patient.

"All I know is that the guy is a CEO of a successful company. He didn't say what it was or what it did."

"Why don't you look him up online?" Jonathan suggested.

"Google a patient? I've never done that. It feels like an invasion of privacy."

"Maybe he has a website. Anything on it would have been put there by him. What he chooses to reveal, and what he doesn't, may help guide you. Is there any psychiatric ethical rule about it?"

Andrea contemplated that as Jonathan rubbed the soles of her feet. "There isn't, but it still doesn't feel right to me. I'll see what I can find out during our next session. I've had tough patients before. Maybe there's a nice person under that obnoxious exterior."

CHAPTER FOUR

NDREA'S NOTIFICATION LIGHT WENT ON AT three minutes before the hour. She opened the door precisely at noon and found Blake Harris, seated on the sofa with a magazine, waiting for his second therapy session. He preceded her into the room.

This time, when he entered her office, he circumnavigated it, apparently attempting to deduce information about her from her environment. She watched him with interest.

Her office was tasteful, tranquil and completely impersonal. A contemporary sofa, large enough for couple's therapy, was upholstered in taupe velvet, as was the comfortable armchair she reserved for herself. One wall had built-in bookcases, but all the books were medical and psychiatric texts.

She had seen to it that there were no personal photographs or accessories. There was an antique fruitwood desk with a closed laptop and a neat pile of papers, tamed with a crystal paperweight. The art consisted of a set of framed botanical prints and two laminated diplomas, one from her medical school at UC San Diego, and the other,

her Residency documentation from the Neuropsychiatric Institute at UCLA.

She suspected he was already aware of her academic credentials. It was time to put a stop to his exploration.

"We can get started as soon as you sit down, Dr. Harris."

He chose a seat directly opposite her chair and stared at her, allowing his eyes to rake over her body, head to toe. She was wearing wide-legged navy pants, a crisp white cotton blouse buttoned up to her collar, and a wide leather belt. Andrea made it a point to dress modestly and professionally at all times.

She noticed him focusing on her hands. Her fingers were long and slim, her nails short with clear polish, and she wore a wide gold wedding band.

"How are you feeling today, Dr. Harris," she said.

"Exhausted."

"Continued nightmares?"

"You haven't cured me yet."

Andrea raised her eyebrows and didn't respond to his bait. "Were you able to remember and write down some of them?"

Blake opened his briefcase and removed a manila file folder. He handed it to her.

"Why don't we look at your notes together?" She removed the papers from the folder and glanced down at them. "I see you've recorded only one dream this past week."

"I don't remember all of them. I just know I've had one when I wake up in a sweat with my heart pounding. My internist insisted I spend a few nights wired up in the sleep lab at Memorial Hospital. Every time I woke suddenly, I'd been in REM sleep with increased blood pressure, pulse and respiration."

Andrea turned her attention to his report. "In this dream, you're lying on a beach. There's a woman next to you and the two of you begin to have sex. Suddenly, you hear a roar and are overcome by a tsunami."

"You can see why they wake me up," he said.

"You're on a tropical beach with a woman. Was she someone you're in a relationship with?"

"Not a sexual relationship."

"But you were having sex with her. Do you have a current sexual partner?"

"I don't have time for relationships. My work keeps me too busy. If I want sex, I hook up on Tinder."

He was watching her face as he said this, perhaps for a sign of disapproval, but she avoided reacting.

"Well, Doc, full disclosure, she was you. What do you think that means?"

Andrea felt a jolt of anxiety. This guy was really blatant. She'd had male patients dream about her before, but rarely did they admit to anything sexual. She hated the way he was coming on to her. Either he was baiting her, or he was dangerous. She kept her expression neutral.

"It's not unusual for a patient to have fantasies about a therapist."

"Yeah, I know, it's called transference. What do you make of the tsunami?"

"Tell me why you think you dreamed of a tsunami."

"Maybe my subconscious was telling me you're off limits." Blake leaned forward and gave her a charming smile. "My internist failed to mention that you're gorgeous."

She didn't respond to his effort at flirtation. "Have you remembered any details about that family dinner you mentioned?

Blake shrugged. "I don't want to talk about my damn family."

"I don't understand," Andrea said. "You came to me to get rid of your nightmares and you're avoiding discussing the dinner that might have triggered them. I thought you'd be anxious to get to the bottom of this as quickly as possible."

"I thought about it. I'm not sure where to begin."

"Why not start by telling me about your relationship with your brother?"

Blake leaned back, hands behind his head. "That's easy. Roger disliked and ignored me. There was no relationship."

"Elaborate on that, please."

"Roger was the heir apparent to my father's business empire and our parents gave him everything he wanted. His first car, at sixteen, was a Mercedes convertible. It made him very popular with the girls. He wasn't all that bright, but he got into USC on the basis of his high school football career and our father's large alumni donations."

"You must have had some interactions as children."

"He considered me a pest and had as little to do with me as possible. I remember asking him for help with my homework once, when I was in the sixth grade. He gave me all the wrong answers, and convinced me that he knew better because he was older. I trusted him and flunked a test. He said that would teach me never to bother him again."

"And did Roger take over the family firm?" Andrea asked.

"As soon as he graduated, Roger fled to New York and got a job there, as far away from our father as he could get. He makes an obligatory visit home every few years and I can usually come up with an excuse not to see him. Of course, once he left and made it clear he wasn't moving back, Dad turned his attentions to me. Roger had been the heir. I was the spare."

"Your father must have been impressed when you became head of a successful company yourself."

"He has grudging admiration for all the money I make,

and is annoyed that I didn't follow his script for me. He disapproved of my interest in science. As you can imagine, I don't see my parents very much."

"But you chose to attend this dinner," Andrea pointed out.

"It was a command performance. My father said Roger had important news to share with the entire family and had particularly requested my presence. Curiosity, rather than brotherly love, prompted me to go. I thought maybe he was announcing his divorce from blonde bimbo number three. It turned out to be more interesting. He wanted to tell everyone that he'd been diagnosed with metastatic prostate cancer, a particularly aggressive form, and that he had failed all the standard therapies."

"I'm sorry to hear that. How did you feel when he told you?"

Blake leaned back again and gave her a chilling smile. "I felt triumphant," he said.

"I don't understand."

"Roger had come home to beg his baby brother to save his life. He knew I was the only person who might be able to help him."

Blake stood up, reaching into his back pocket for his wallet. He extracted a business card and handed it to her.

"Why don't you look me up and see if you can figure out why Roger came to me? I'd like you to know more about what I do and who I am. It will save time if you learn about my professional life online. That way, we can focus on what's really important when we're in session. I'll be interested to see what you think of my work. I'm proud of it."

"From what you've said, I assume your company creates new drugs."

"We do. We specialize in Cancer Immune therapy and we've had a major research breakthrough."

"In treating prostate cancer?"

"You got it. I don't want to waste my time explaining it in detail, assuming you can figure it out yourself."

"I'd much prefer you to explain your work to me in your own words. If your work is important to you, it won't waste your time to tell me about it. We can discuss it when I see you next week."

Blake shrugged, and walked out.

After the door closed, Andrea glanced at the card before tucking it into the pocket of her slacks.

Blake Harris PhD, CEO
Chess Pharmaceuticals.

Tempting as it might be to look him up online, she knew it would be a mistake. He was clearly testing her, trying to take control of their sessions and challenging her to fitness to be his therapist.

CHAPTER FIVE

ANDREA WAS GRATEFUL THAT HER ONE O'CLOCK patient was out of town. Her stomach was growling and she didn't do her most insightful therapy on an empty stomach.

When she went into the utility room, she found Charles Davis, her office mate, in front of the microwave. He gave her a warm smile as she removed her lunch from the refrigerator.

Charles was the most handsome seventy-five-year-old man she knew. He was also a brilliant therapist and she was thankful every day that he had become her mentor and supervisor. Charles was tall and slim, with a runner's body that had made him a college track star. He had an untamed head of curly white hair, bushy eyebrows, and wore his glasses halfway down his patrician nose. The best thing about having Charles as her supervisor was that there was no ethical conflict in discussing her hostile new patient with him.

"Care to join me for lunch?" he said, removing his lasagna from the microwave.

"Your office or mine?" Andrea opened a can of Diet Sprite and unwrapped her tuna sandwich.

"Mine, I think. Yours is always so neat, I worry about getting lasagna on your velvet upholstery."

Charles's large oak desk was covered in piles of charts and paper, his bookcase stuffed with reference texts, hard copy journals, and knick-knacks. The walls were covered with museum posters and his many degrees and honors.

Andrea put her sandwich and drink on the coffee table and sunk into the cushions of his elderly, cracked black leather sofa. Charles took his place opposite her on his reclining chair.

"You look a bit agitated," he said. "Difficult session?"

"There's something bothering me about this new patient. I can usually deal with arrogance, hostility, and distrust. What I'm having trouble with is my feeling that underneath the clean-cut smart aleck is something even more creepy."

"Why is he in therapy?"

"If I can believe what he says, it's because his internist has run out of options and is making him see me. He's got severe insomnia due to recurrent nightmares, all of which have to do with water."

"What does he think the dreams are about?"

"He won't say. I suspect he thinks therapy is a game that he'll win, if he doesn't reveal anything and keeps me guessing. It's almost as if he wants to prove I'm not smart enough to help him."

"How do you react to that?"

"On the surface, I maintain my calm, listen attentively and ask open-ended questions. Inside my head, I feel like I'm running out of patience and have to restrain myself from replying with a put down."

"It isn't like you to feel angry with a patient. You usually manage to find something to like even in the most difficult ones. It's the part of them that you focus on, when you attempt to help them."

Andrea sipped her drink while she searched for a response. "Maybe the problem is that I can't find anything to like about this man."

"What does he do for a living?"

"He's the CEO of a company that developed a new immune therapy drug for prostate cancer."

"Why don't you get him started talking about his company. You know how we men enjoy bragging about our accomplishments. Maybe it will loosen him up and give you another perspective on who he is."

"I'm glad you think so, but I have to tell you, the more I treat the guy, the more he gives me the creeps."

"What kind of creeps? Exactly how does he make you feel?"

Andrea chewed on her lower lip and gave the question some serious thought. "I think there's some element of fear. This guy's eyes are ice cold. When he looks at me, I'm not sure if he's wanting to control me, evaluating me as a bedmate, or just hates me."

"Or all of the above?" Charles asked.

"My intuition is usually reliable when I reach out to a patient and formulate a treatment plan, but I can't read him. He seems to be pushing me to challenge him, and I feel like I'm walking on eggs, trying to do that in a way that doesn't cause him to lash out. In all honesty, he makes me angry, and I'm finding it hard to treat someone I dislike so much."

"Has he made any overt sexual overtures to you?"

"He described a nightmare in which he was having sex with me on a beach and was caught in a tsunami, and he told me I was gorgeous. He also makes a point of looking at me, head to toe, when he comes in."

"How did you handle all of that?"

Andrea shrugged. "I just commented that it isn't unusual for a patient to have fantasies about a therapist and changed the subject, but truthfully, it made me very anxious."

"Are you worried that he'll continue to come on to you, sexually?"

"I wouldn't be surprised. He's very controlling. I'm not looking forward to dealing with it."

"Do you think this man is treatable? Can you help him?"

"I don't know. My instinct tells me that if I can get to the bottom of those dreams, and help him deal with whatever his subconscious is hiding, I might be able to. That's a big 'if' with such a resistant patient. I sense he doesn't take any of it seriously."

"Do you want to help him?"

"I want to give it my best shot. You know me, Charles. I never back down from a challenge. In any case, we only have two more sessions before he decides whether I'm productive enough to continue being paid."

____

CHAPTER SIX

WHEN BLAKE HARRIS RETURNED TO HIS OFFICE at Chess Pharmaceuticals, he told the receptionist he wanted to see George, his very productive laboratory director, immediately. When he started his company, four years ago, he'd rented office and laboratory space from another, older, start-up company. The space was now too small for the next steps he needed to take, human clinical trials and marketing his breakthrough drug, Blakimab. It was time for a decision.

There was a knock on his door and George entered.

"I've got the results of the next round of animal studies, sir," he said.

George's expression told his boss that the results were excellent.

Blake took the paperwork from George and perused the graphs, nodding as they exceeded his expectations. Their genetically engineered mice had been inoculated with very aggressive, hormone resistant, prostate cancer cells, and once the tumor was well established, treated with their experimental drug. Seventy percent of them had complete remission and the remainder had a partial response.

"Good work," Blake said.

"Shall I set up the next set of appointments with the drug companies?" George asked. "Pfizer, Bayer and Genentech were very impressed with our initial data at the first meetings. I think this follow-up data should seal the deal, and put us in a perfect negotiation position."

"I've decided not to sell. We should get a big infusion of venture capital and expand. This could be a blockbuster drug."

"It could, and you would probably make more money independently if it were, but I thought you weren't interested in clinical trials and marketing. I thought you wanted to focus on drug design. You could sell this one for more than enough to pay off your initial investors, start a new company to develop a different drug, and still be very rich while avoiding the tedious part."

"You're forgetting that I'd have to commit to staying with them and seeing the process through for several years. They aren't just buying the drug. They want the mind that developed it, in hopes that I hand them the next blockbuster. I'm not letting anyone be my boss."

"It's your call, of course, Dr. Harris, but you still might want to meet again with each of them and get their best offer. In the meantime, I could contact some of the bigger venture capital firms with this data and see how much they might be willing to loan us for expansion. An offer from one of the big firms would help us raise the money."

"You're right, as usual. Make it so." Blake said.

When George left, Blake sat back in his chair, closed his eyes, and visualized his therapist. She was wearing a gold band, so she was married. That shouldn't be an impediment. He rather liked his sex playmates to be married. It meant they couldn't be jealous of any of his other women, and wouldn't be pressuring him for some kind of commitment. He found the deceit exciting; all that sneaking around in hotels and making sure they weren't seen by any of her friends. Of course, Doctor Andrea presented a special seduction challenge. Shrinks weren't supposed to get involved with their patients.

CHAPTER SEVEN

O N SATURDAY MORNINGS, DESPITE HIS RECENT fatigue, Blake liked to run. The vigorous exercise kept him alert. His favorite route took him around the UCLA campus, up Hilgard Avenue, across on Sunset, where there was actually a track, and down Gayley, where he could stop at Whole Foods for breakfast and pick up a few groceries to carry home. One of the perks of this particular route was the presence of nubile co-eds. Blake enjoyed watching their tight muscled legs, their bouncing breasts and their cute asses. If he saw one who particularly appealed to him, he'd keep pace with her, occasionally follow her to a campus coffee spot, and attempt a pick-up. He could be charming, when he wanted to be. This morning, however, the track had been almost deserted.

It was close to 8:00 a.m. when he reached Whole Foods and sat down with a cup of black coffee, a bowl of whole grain hot cereal, and began reading a discarded section of the Los Angeles Times. As he peered over the edge of his paper, he spotted his psychiatrist.

Andrea wheeled a shopping cart, with Molly seated in the front, from the parking lot into Whole Foods. Molly loved grocery shopping and made sure her mother purchased the correct breakfast cereal and her favorite brand of peanut butter. Andrea was wearing a pair of skinny jeans and a black sweatshirt jacket. Her long hair was up in a ponytail which swung as she walked.

She helped herself to mixed salad greens, fondled the heirloom tomatoes, found a ripe avocado, and collected several apples and baskets of fresh berries. She reached the back of the store and turned into the dairy section where she selected a few gourmet cheeses and two half-gallons of milk. Rounding the corner, she put an organic chicken and some ground lamb into her cart. As she walked up the prepared food aisle to the checkout counter, she noticed a man who reminded her of her least favorite patient. His back was toward her and he was reading a section of the newspaper.

When he spotted Andrea walking up the prepared food aisle, Blake had turned his chair so that she could only see his back, and watched for her reflection in the store window as she approached the checkout line. The store wasn't crowded and it wouldn't take her long. Quickly finishing the last of his coffee, he left and headed to the parking lot. He wanted to see what kind of car she was driving. If she shopped at this particular Whole Foods, she must live in the neighborhood.

There weren't more than a dozen cars at that hour. He was betting that she drove the silver Lexus SUV. It seemed like a perfect young mother car. He stationed himself behind a column, where he had a wide angle view, and waited.

A few minutes later, she emerged and popped the trunk lid on a black Porsche Panamera. He was impressed. He wouldn't have thought she had that kind of good taste. She opened the back door, lifted her child out of the shopping cart, and strapped her into her car seat. He had a nice view of her ass, as she bent to transfer groceries into the trunk. He made a mental note of the license plate number as she drove off.

As he walked home, he hoped that Saturday morning shopping was her regular routine. Perhaps next weekend, he would take his car to the supermarket and follow her home. He wanted to know where his therapist lived.

CHAPTER EIGHT

"Have you ever heard of Chess Pharmaceuticals?" Andrea asked Jonathan, as he helped her put away the groceries.

"Should I have?"

"They're developing a new immune therapy drug for prostate cancer. I don't know anything about the basis of immune therapy. Can you give me a quick education?"

Jonathan helped himself to an apple. "Is there some reason for your sudden interest in prostate cancer?"

"It's my new patient. He handed me his business card, told me to look him up, and challenged me to figure out what he does."

"Did you look him up?"

"Of course not. If I follow his instructions, then he's the boss of our therapy sessions. I can't let that happen. I told him he had to explain his work to me in his own words. I just want to know enough so I don't appear ignorant when he tells me."

Jonathan grinned at her. "You got it. Immunology 101."

She walked over and deposited a kiss on his lips. He tasted like apple juice. He pulled her into a hug.

"Let's finish what we're doing and then I'll make you a snack," she offered.

Fifteen minutes later, with two coffees and a Danish Pastry in hand, Andrea walked into the den. "So, let's hear it. Dumb it down for me. I'm only a psychiatrist."

"Remember T cells from medical school?" he said.

"Of course. They're the white cells that are supposed kill off cancer cells, except they don't."

"Exactly. This past year, two guys got a Nobel prize for figuring out how T cells work. It turns out, it takes three simultaneous actions to kill a cancer cell. First, the T cell has to attach itself to the cancer cell. Then, it has to turn on a protein you can think of as the kill switch. The kill switch is necessary for the T cell to destroy the cancer cell."

"So why doesn't it?"

"That's the fascinating thing. There are also protein brakes, called checkpoints, designed to stop the T cell so it doesn't accidentally destroy a normal cell. Cancer is good at mimicking normal and turning on the brake. The guys who got the Nobel figured out a way to block the brake and give the kill switch free reign."

"Do you think my patient developed a drug that blocks the brake for prostate cancer?"

"It's more complicated. The first generation of these drugs, which are called Checkpoint Inhibitors, worked with cancers like melanoma, or some of the blood cancers that I treat, but they don't work well on solid tumors, such as prostate cancer. Then, researchers discovered that there was more than one brake protein, which generated a whole other series of drugs. If your patient has developed a check-point inhibitor that works for prostate cancer, either he's discovered a new checkpoint, or he's managed to synthesize a drug that attacks more than one at a time. I'll be interested in hearing what he tells you, if you can share it. I know you're walking a fine line here."

"Thanks, darling," Andrea said. "That's really helpful. I can't wait to hear what he's going to say at our next session."

Andrea finished her coffee and Danish, and turned to Jonathan again. "You know, I haven't heard from Hannah lately. I thought she and Daniel were back from their honeymoon by now."

"Maybe they're just adjusting to being newlyweds. You remember how that was?"

"They've been living together for years and they bought a house and got pregnant before the wedding. One wouldn't think it was that much of an adjustment."

"Maybe Hannah's too busy throwing up to call her friends."

"Maybe. I think I should call her and make sure she's okay."

"Why don't you invite them all for a family dinner next weekend? Jonathan suggested.

Andrea gave him a thumbs up sign, and left the den for her study.

Sitting at her desk, she took out her cell phone and called Hannah. She hoped her best friend wasn't suffering too much from first trimester symptoms.

She and Hannah had met at an Emily's List event five years ago and Andrea found her smart, funny and a good listener. Both of them were very private, and it had taken awhile for enough trust to develop to exchange confidences. When Andrea became pregnant with Molly, she'd asked Hannah to take care of her. When Hannah met and fell in love with Detective Daniel Ross of the LAPD, Andrea was her sounding board. Last month, Andrea had, at Hannah's request, become ordained online and officiated at their wedding.

"Hi, sweetie. When did you and Daniel get back?"

"About a week ago. Sorry I haven't called. It's been hectic."

"How was the honeymoon?"

There was period of silence.

Then Hannah's voice cracked. "It was awful. The day after we got there, the chef at the B&B was murdered. But that's not the worst of it."

"What else?" Andrea asked.

"It's too complicated for a phone call. I'll tell you when I see you."

"I actually called to invite you all over next weekend for a family dinner. Would you rather drop Zoe off here tomorrow and have a girls' afternoon, so we can talk?"

"That sounds good. I'm still processing, but you know how I value your input. Tomorrow actually works out better," Hannah said. "Daniel and I are both on call next weekend, so dinner would have been dicey."

"Come over around noon. We'll feed the girls lunch and leave them in Jonathan's capable hands."

CHAPTER NINE

ONE LOOK AT HANNAH AND ANDREA WAS worried. She was dressed in sweats and sneakers, her long red hair up in a messy bun, and was wearing no makeup. There were dark circles around her eyes. Hannah dressed for comfort rather than fashion, but she was always well groomed and professional, even on weekends. She didn't look like a happy newlywed.

"Aunt Andrea!" Zoe, her brown eyes sparkling, and her curly dark hair haloing her face, held up her arms for a hug.

Andrea bent down and picked her up. "Molly can't wait to see you."

Zoe had adopted Molly as her little sister and took the responsibility seriously. As Molly appeared in the hall, Zoe ran to her, took her by the hand, and followed her into the kitchen.

"Jonathan is babysitting," Andrea said. "We have the afternoon for girl talk. Want to retreat to my study with hot chocolate and some lunch, or take a walk?"

Hannah rolled her eyes. "Hot chocolate trumps exercise every time."

Hannah headed in the direction of the study, and Andrea, having anticipated her choice, stopped in the kitchen for a tray of peanut butter cookies, tuna sandwiches, and two mugs of chocolate. Setting it down on the coffee table, she deposited herself next to her friend on the sofa.

"Do you serve cookies to your patients?" Hannah asked, biting into one.

"Only the nicest ones. Tell me what's going on, sweetie."

Hannah finished chewing, washed the bite down with a sip of chocolate, and took a deep breath. "I lost the pregnancy."

Andrea reached over and took her hand. "Hannah, I'm so sorry. I know how long it took, going through IVF."

"Every time I see Zoe with Molly, I think about what a great big sister she would be, and I just want to cry."

"She still can be a big sister. Don't you have embryos left?"

"I do, but that isn't the issue. I'm not sure I want to stay married to Daniel. I haven't told you everything that happened on our honeymoon. It's a mess."

Andrea waited.

"Daniel made reservations at a B&B on an island he'd visited when he was in the military, stationed at Fort Lewis. It turned out that the owner was a woman he'd had a one night stand with, just before he was discharged."

"That was a long time ago," Andrea said. "Were you jealous? You know Daniel adores you."

"Daniel and I never talked much about past sexual relationships. Ben was my one and only, and Daniel was my first after Ben died. I assumed he'd slept with other women, before and after his first wife. The problem..." Hannah's eyes filled with tears.

Andrea reached over and hugged her.

"The problem," said Hannah, wiping at her tears with

her fingers, "is that his one night stand got pregnant. It turns out Daniel has a 13-year-old son named Josh. Not only that, but Daniel was married to Annie when he had that one night stand. How can I trust him now?"

"Did Daniel know about his son?" Andrea was astonished. She'd always read Daniel as a straight arrow, not as a guy capable of cheating on his wife. Where were her well honed therapeutic instincts?

"No, of course not. He was as shocked as I was when he found out, but he wants to have a relationship with his son, and pay child support."

"What's his son like?"

"He seems like a nice kid. I could deal with the two of them having a relationship, if I hadn't just lost our baby." She broke into tears again. "I've had so many patients have miscarriages, and I always try to be empathic, but I didn't realize until now how much it hurts, and how real that baby is, even when it's just a first trimester fetus. You've already decorated the nursery in your head, applied to pre-school and started saving for college, and then it's gone."

"Oh, sweetheart. At least he's taking responsibility and offering financial help. That's the right thing to do."

Hannah nodded. "Yeah, he gets credit for that, but what about his cheating?"

"Did you ask him about it?"

Hannah shook her head. "I was too upset about everything else that happened. We were in the middle of trying to solve a murder."

"Did you solve it?"

"Of course. We're very good at detecting together. I'm just not sure anymore if we'll be good at being married. How am I going to tell Zoe about this?"

"I think telling Zoe is Daniel's responsibility. She might

like the idea of having a big brother. It's not as if he's going to live with you."

"That's true. I just don't know what to do next. I had a D&C in the office Monday morning and went back to the office on Tuesday. It took me a whole morning to excavate my desk, and my schedule was totally full because I'd been away. I was too exhausted to think about it, or to talk to Daniel. He was also swamped with work this past week, but I know he went to see his lawyer."

"Hannah, I wouldn't make any decisions yet," Andrea said. "You and Daniel have been together for several years and you've been very happy. Don't throw it away without giving him a chance to explain himself, and seeing what you can work out going forward. He's never given you any reason to think that the man he is now wouldn't be faithful to you."

"I haven't been able to talk about any of this until now. He and I have been walking on eggshells around one another."

"You have to talk to one another. There's no other way to deal with this."

"I know," Hannah sighed. "But I just haven't had enough emotional energy to get up the courage."

Andrea reached out and held Hannah's hand, feeling as if she too wanted to cry. Compared to what Hannah had been through over the past two weeks, her own upset about her difficult patient seemed trivial. This was an afternoon when she knew she needed to listen and not complain.

CHAPTER TEN

B LAKE ARRIVED PRECISELY ON TIME AND GAVE Andrea a cheery smile when she greeted him in the waiting room.

"So, Doctor," he said as he seated himself, leaning forward to engage her, "what did you make of my business card?"

"It didn't tell me anything you haven't already mentioned. You're the CEO of a pharmaceutical start-up company. Would you like to tell me something about the drug you've developed?"

"You didn't look me up?" He seemed annoyed that she hadn't followed his directions.

"I told you I wouldn't," Andrea said. "Even with your permission, looking up a patient online strays into gray ethical territory. I am, however, very interested in hearing about your drug because it is so important to you."

"Do you know anything about immunotherapy?"

"A little. I recently read an article about the two guys who won the Nobel Prize for discovering Checkpoint Inhibitors. Is that the kind of drug you developed?"

"We created a new drug called Blakimab. It inhibits two checkpoints simultaneously. We've given rats an aggressive strain of prostate cancer and achieved remarkable remissions."

"Well, it's certainly clear why your brother sought you out. Did he want you to give him your drug, even before it gets approved for human use by the FDA?"

"Bravo. I didn't know psychiatrists knew anything about cancer research."

She shrugged. "I try to keep up with cutting edge medicine, and a great deal of it, since the human genome was deciphered, is in cancer. Is there any way you can help your brother?"

"The drug hasn't even gone into human clinical trials yet. I can't just give it to him. An oncologist would have to agree to administer it, and we'd have to submit an application to the FDA for Compassionate Use. That means there are no other treatment options available. Could I help him? Maybe. Do I want to? Not really."

"Because...?"

"Because Roger is a bastard. Did I tell you he drowned my cat?"

"No."

"When I was a kid, I had a black and white tuxedo cat named Sylvester. Roger hated it. One day, I found my cat dead in our pool. Sylvester was strictly an indoor cat, and he hated water. He'd run every time I turned the faucet on. Roger never missed an opportunity to frighten him."

"So, quid pro quo. You believe that he arranged for your cat to die, so you'd let Roger die, even though you might be able to save him."

"It's not the same, Doctor. Killing Sylvester required planning and execution. Not going to the trouble of cutting through a mountain of red tape, to give my brother my experimental drug, simply requires me to do nothing. Roger's not my responsibility."

"Perhaps there's a connection between your brother's visit, your drowned cat, and your nightmares," Andrea said.

"Look, Doc, before we take this any further, I owe you an apology. I've been acting like an ass in here; arguing with you, baiting you and testing you. My rational brain knows you're only trying to help."

"Do you have any idea about why you felt angry with me?" She didn't believe in the sincerity of his apology. Her instincts told her he had an ulterior motive.

He gave her his most disarming smile. "Honestly, I think I was scared. You seem to be my last resort, dealing with all this, and I was trying to see if you were smart enough to help me. If I had concluded you weren't, and I got nowhere, I could blame you, rather than myself."

"That's pretty insightful, Dr. Harris."

"Please, call me Blake. I had another bad week. I'm finding it hard to concentrate on data. I'm falling asleep in the middle of the afternoon in my office. My brain feels fuzzy. You are clearly smart enough to help me, and frankly, I'm relieved. I'll try and be a better patient going forward."

"It sounds as if you're ready to make some real progress."

"I am ready to make progress," Blake replied, leaning forward. "I've been thinking...you get to ask me all kinds of personal questions in therapy, but I don't know anything about you, other than where you got your degrees. Are you married, Doc? Kids?"

"Therapy is all about you, Blake. Your experiences, your problems, your feelings. It's not a social conversation in which it's impolite to fail to inquire about the other person's life."

"So, you're not going to answer my question?"

"No." He was testing her again, seeing if he could disarm

her with charm and then push the boundaries. Fortunately, this was a game with which she was quite familiar. "Why don't we continue where we left off? Tell me some more details about the dinner."

"Sure. It was the end of September and warm. We ate outside by the pool and my father showed off his skills at the barbeque. The menu was Caesar Salad, mashed potatoes and prime sirloin steak. Naturally, I couldn't eat any of it. I'm vegan. Are you vegan, Doc? If you aren't, you should be. It's better for your health."

Andrea ignored his question. "Did your parents know you were vegan when they asked you to come to dinner?"

"I mentioned it to my father, but as far as he's concerned, his kids have to eat whatever he chooses to serve. I had to go into the kitchen and fix myself a salad without all that cheese and without egg in the dressing. I was pissed. Naturally, Roger ate everything and sucked up to our father."

"Your parents must have been very upset about your brother's illness," Andrea said.

Blake didn't appear to be the least bit concerned. "Hard to tell. They're both the masters of the poker face. My father did say that, of course, Blake would make his new drug available to his big brother. You should have seen his face when I told him I didn't think it was possible. He slammed his fist on the table and said 'you make it happen, you little shit.' Very inspiring."

"Have you had any second thoughts on the subject?"

"As a matter of fact, I told George, my laboratory chief, that a patient had approached me about being our experimental subject. I didn't tell him it was my brother. George thought we should do it. If we save his life, it would mean a huge infusion of capital to expand the company and do the clinical trials ourselves, or it would raise our value if I decide to sell. I hadn't considered that aspect of Roger's request."

"The drug might not work, and Roger could die anyway," Andrea pointed out.

"I wouldn't shed any tears over Roger, but I wouldn't be happy about the financial consequences. I don't think that will happen. I've got great confidence in my drug. I haven't made up my mind yet, but I'm thinking about it. By the way, I think you're right about Roger and my nightmares. I had the first one the night after the dinner. Roger was drowning in our pool. I was a kid, and I just stood there and watched. You probably think I wanted to save him, and felt helpless because I was just a kid, but I remember feeling glad, like he deserved to drown."

"In the other nightmares you've described to me, you were the one in danger of drowning, and you experienced terror that woke you. This one seems different."

Blake considered for awhile. "You're right. I don't recall being frightened after the first dream. That started later."

"I'm afraid we're about out of time," she said. "It appears we'll have a great deal to talk about at your next session."

Blake rose from the sofa. "See you next week, Doc."

Andrea was relieved that it was Friday and she had a weekend to decompress. The image of Blake's drowned cat made the hair rise on the back of her neck. Perhaps it was because Molly was continuing to beg for a kitten, and clearly, she and Jonathan were going to give in.

CHAPTER ELEVEN

THE NEXT MORNING, BLAKE DROVE TO WHOLE Foods. He took his Range Rover, figuring that the Maserati would be too conspicuous in the parking lot. He arrived early, did some grocery shopping, grabbed a large black coffee to go, and returned to his car. He'd parked with a view to the store entrance, but far enough back so that he was unlikely to be seen. He took out his phone, attached a pair of ear buds, and found some classical music to listen to as he sipped his coffee. He'd give it half an hour. He was going to see what else he could dig up about Andrea's private life. He'd rarely met a woman he found so attractive and so intellectually worthy of him. He was going to mount a charm offensive and make her want him.

Andrea's car arrived promptly at 8:15 a.m. This time she was alone, wearing gray tights, knee-high boots, and a long, dark green sweater. Her sexy long hair was loose. The tights showed off shapely legs and he imagined pulling them down and touching what was beneath them. He could return to the store and accidentally run into her, but he'd rather find out where she lived.

He waited patiently for her to shop, put her groceries in the car, and drive to the exit, staying far enough behind so that she wouldn't notice him. He followed her through the residential streets until he saw her turn into a driveway. Pulling up and stopping at the curb, he waited a few minutes to be certain she had time to enter her house, then drove slowly past it. The house was an original 1920s Spanish Revival with a drought-friendly garden of succulents. There was a tiled staircase leading to the carved oak front door and a garage at ground level. He made note of the address.

Homes in this neighborhood were worth a great deal of money. Her husband must be doing well. He couldn't imagine her affording this house on what a psychiatrist could earn. He'd need to find out her husband's name and something about him.

He pulled up in front of a neighbor's home, aware that he couldn't stay there long because he lacked a residential parking permit, but he was hoping she might leave the house again. Luck was with him. Twenty minutes later, an SUV emerged from the garage, driven by a man with dark hair. Andrea was in the passenger seat, and he glimpsed the child in a car seat behind them. They turned left, and drove past him. He waited a few moments, made a U-turn, and followed.

The SUV turned right on Wilshire, left on Westwood, and pulled into the parking lot of a Petco store. Blake followed them, parking in a different row. Andrea's husband exited the car first. He was tall and good looking, wearing a gray sweatshirt and matching sweatpants. He opened the back door, leaned in and emerged with the little blonde girl, whom he carried. Andrea exited the other side, located a shopping cart, and the three of them disappeared into the store.

Blake stared after them. No point in following them inside. He needed to see Andrea alone. He wondered what kind of a pet they had. No matter. He'd find another way. He wondered what her relationship was like with her husband. Just because he was good-looking didn't mean he was hot in bed, or even as financially successful as Blake was. He'd figure out what she wasn't getting at home and provide it for her. Women with small children needed some excitement in their lives.

Andrea pushed her shopping cart into Petco, wondering if she was going to regret this decision. Between her patients and her family, her bandwidth for nurturing was minimal. At least cats didn't need to be walked.

"Mommy, where do they keep the kitties?" Molly asked.

"There aren't any here, sweetie. This is the kitty supply store. We can't bring a kitty home unless we have food for it and a bed."

"And toys?"

"Yes, toys." Andrea added one more thing to her mental list. She found the aisle for cat supplies and Jonathan followed directions, placing items in the cart: wet and dry cat food, kitty litter, one of those fancy self cleaning litter containers, a bed, bowls, a carrying case and a scratching post to distract the cat from the furniture. She put Molly in charge of picking out a few toys.

They paid for their purchases and loaded them into the back of the SUV.

"Let's go get my kitty now." Molly demanded.

"We will," Andrea said.

"What if they don't have any?" Jonathan whispered.

Andrea rolled her eyes. "I called ahead. They've got a ten-week-old litter of five kittens."

The woman at the front desk of the West Los Angeles Animal Adoption Center was very welcoming. The moment she spotted Molly, she knew she'd be able to place a pet. She led them into a back room full of cages. Several dogs barked and jumped excitedly as they entered.

"I want a dog, too." Molly said.

"Not today, sweetheart," Jonathan said. "Today is kitten day."

Molly turned her attention away from a black Labrador with soulful chocolate eyes and followed them. At the back of the room was a cage full of kittens, curled into a single ball. Three of them were calico, two were black.

"Would you like to pet one?" the receptionist asked Molly. "Come and sit down."

Molly sat obediently in the proffered chair, as the woman removed one of the calico cats from the cage and placed it gently in Molly's lap. Molly began to stroke her, and the kitten climbed up her shirt and settled herself on Molly's shoulder, purring loudly.

"She likes me, Mommy."

"Do you like her?"

Molly grinned. "I love her. Can I have her?"

Andrea and Jonathan exchanged glances. It appeared a decision had been made.

Soon, with the cat ensconced in her carrying case next to Molly, they headed home.

"I want to show her to Zoe," Molly announced.

"Not this weekend," Andrea said. "Auntie Hannah and Uncle Daniel are both on call."

CHAPTER TWELVE

I T WAS UNUSUAL FOR HANNAH AND DANIEL TO both be on call the same weekend. Hannah alternated weekends with her partner, Ruth. Daniel was one of six detective teams, so that both his night and weekend calls were fewer.

Hannah took Zoe with her to Memorial Hospital in the mornings, to make rounds. The nurses always made a fuss over her, and the patients loved meeting Hannah's "physician's assistant." Zoe was the only kid in her class who got to watch Mommy take out surgical staples and see lots of newborn babies.

In the afternoons, Hannah arranged play dates for her, and paid Emilia overtime to sleep in all three nights, in case she and Daniel were both called out simultaneously. Saturday afternoon and evening were taken up with two deliveries and one gang shooting. Sunday was quiet so far, and Hannah found herself alone in the house with Daniel for the first time that week.

She'd been thinking about what to say to him, and how to say it. The problem was that her feelings were still a confused mess of hurt, anger and loss, and she had no idea what his half of the conversation would be like. When she walked in, she found him on the deck, staring out into space.

"A dollar for your thoughts," she said.

He turned towards her. "Allowing for inflation? I'm not sure they're worth a dollar. I was just remembering our wedding, out here. Hard to believe it was only three weeks ago. Too much has happened, and I've been trying to figure out how to talk to you about it."

Hannah sat down on the lounge chair opposite him. "I haven't been in a very talkative mood since we got back. I didn't know what to say. Did you see your lawyer?"

Daniel nodded. "He's drawing up an agreement. I want to set up a college account for Josh, and pay Melanie child support going forward. In return, I'm asking to spend time with him. I told the attorney not to do that part of the agreement until I had a chance to talk to you about it."

Hannah wondered if that was true. Did he really care how she felt, or was he just pretending to want her approval about the arrangements? "What kind of time did you have in mind?"

"I'd like him to come down for a week during his winter and spring breaks from school, and to spend at least two weeks of his summer vacation with us. I'd also like to be able to go up for occasional weekends, and take him hiking or camping in the Northwest. Would that be okay with you?"

"Daniel, I'm not sure I'm ready to have him visit over Christmas vacation. It's too soon. We just lost our child and now you want me to forget all about that, and accept a teenager you knew nothing about into our family."

Daniel got up and stood behind her, massaging the tight muscles in her shoulders and neck. "Don't you think that I'm sad about your miscarriage too? I was thrilled when you got pregnant. Having Josh as your stepson doesn't mean we can't try again. Besides, there's no way that agreement will be signed and sealed before this winter's school break. If I read Melanie correctly, she's going to negotiate for all she can get."

"What about Zoe? You have to tell her about this. I can't think of how to do that, and I don't want to."

Daniel's hands stilled and he returned to his chair.

She wiped her face before he could notice that she'd been crying.

"I will tell Zoe. I promise, but not until I'm sure Josh can visit. Melanie may fight me on that. She didn't even want me to know Josh existed. I know she needs the money and is entitled to it, but she might take me to court to forbid contact. It could take awhile to sort all this out, and I don't want to promise Zoe a big brother I can't deliver."

That made sense. Part of her wished Melanie would take Daniel to court and win. That way she wouldn't have to deal with his youthful mistake. On the other hand, she had to give him credit for doing the right thing, and Josh did seem like a nice kid. None of this was his fault.

"Daniel, I don't know if I have the emotional energy to try again, even if we do still have a few viable embryos left."

Daniel didn't say anything for awhile.

Finally, he took a deep breath and sighed. "Sweetheart, we're both hurt and grieving, and confused about all of this. Let's not make any premature decisions. I know having IVF was difficult for you, and Louise's murder made it a nightmare. Can we agree to allow things to settle down for a few months, and revisit it when we're calmer and less depressed?"

Hannah nodded. There was one more thing she had to get off her chest. "The thing about Josh that bothers me the most, is that he was conceived while you were married to

Annie. It would feel different to me if you'd been single. How can I trust you won't cheat on me?"

She stared at him with a tight jawed expression on her face.

"Hannah, that was fourteen years ago. Annie and I were separated by my military service, and when we saw one another, all we did was argue. She was so angry that I'd decided not to be a lawyer and had actually volunteered for the army. She thought I'd done it to get away from her."

"Had you?"

"I mostly wanted to get away from my parents, who were equally annoyed at me. I didn't know what I wanted to do with my life, and everyone around me was critical of my decisions. The military seemed like a foolproof escape."

"Good thing we weren't fighting any wars at the time," Hannah commented.

"I knew that Melanie was a big mistake as soon as it was over. I felt very guilty. Annie didn't deserve my infidelity. I tried my best, after I was discharged, to make things work between us, but they didn't. I realize I have to earn back your trust, but believe me, the only woman I want is you."

He sounded sincere, but actions were more important than words, so she would have to see how he behaved going forward.

"Okay, why don't you tell your lawyer to negotiate for the time you want, and we'll let everything else go for the time being."

Daniel looked relieved.

Andrea would be proud of her, actually managing to initiate an honest conversation with Daniel. Hannah wondered if Andrea would suggest that the two of them go into marital therapy.

CHAPTER THIRTEEN

THE FOLLOWING MONDAY, BLAKE MADE UP HIS mind about Roger. The financial incentive was too great and Roger was a willing guinea pig. He called George into his office and gave him instructions.

"I want you to run a series of experiments designed to determine the optimum dose of Blakimab in milligrams, per gram of rat. I'm assuming that once we exceed the optimum dose, we'll begin to see complications. If we're going to do a human experiment, we need to know how much stuff to use."

"I doubt that the ratio of drug to rat, and that of drug to human, will be the same," George said.

"We have to start somewhere. I'm going to tell the patient I'm willing to apply to the FDA for compassionate use, if he'll come out here and be treated by an oncologist of my choice, so I can follow him closely. I'll start contacting the best oncologists in town. One more thing you should know. This patient is my older brother."

"Seriously, sir? Do you want to take the risk that the drug might kill him?"

Blake shrugged. "He's going to die anyway, without it. If we succeed, it's a win for both of us. If the drug fails, what has he got left to lose?"

"I understand," George said. "I'll get started."

Blake picked up the phone and called his brother.

"What made you change your mind?" Roger said.

"Brotherly love," said Blake. "I'm going to recruit an oncologist to work with us if the application is approved. Plan to move back into your old room for a few months."

"I'd rather die right now. I'll be renting a bungalow at the Beverly Hills Hotel."

Blake laughed and hung up. He appreciated the sentiment.

Turning to his computer, he logged on to the Memorial Hospital website and searched for oncologists. He knew that Memorial Hematology Oncology was the largest and most prestigious group practice. He looked up the individual members, checking out their academic credentials and research interests, hoping to find someone on the cutting edge of prostate cancer research who would be tempted by his offer.

Suddenly, he did a double-take. The photo of Dr. Jonathan Marcus, an expert in leukemia and lymphoma, caught his attention. That had to be Andrea's husband. How interesting it would be to collaborate with one of his partners, and perhaps insinuate himself into Jonathan's life. At the very least, he'd have an information source close to the Marcus family. Being married to an oncologist certainly explained Andrea's impressive familiarity with cancer research.

He identified a possible collaborator for his drug study in the Memorial group, and two others at alternate institutions, but no point in jumping the gun. He needed permission first. Printing out the appropriate forms from the FDA website, he began the tedious task of filling out the paperwork. He wondered what Andrea would say when he told her what he'd decided about Roger.

CHAPTER FOURTEEN

"GOOD AFTERNOON, BLAKE," ANDREA SAID.

She was wearing a loose, dark green cashmere poncho and matching slacks. She disliked the way Blake scanned her when she walked in, and this outfit concealed her shape.

"How was your week?"

"Interesting," Blake said. "I have a number of things to tell you."

She waited for him to proceed.

"I changed my mind about Roger. I've submitted the application for compassionate use, and he's agreed to come here for treatment with the oncologist of my choice."

"What made you change your mind?" she asked.

"I needed a first human experimental subject for my drug and he volunteered. I would have accepted anyone else, so it didn't make sense to turn down my brother. Roger's going to die anyway, so I figure he has nothing to lose. If my drug fails, he might die sooner, and if it works, he'll die later."

What an ice cold response. Andrea worked at keeping her face from showing the repulsion she felt at his answer.

"Right now, I'd rather spend our time talking about my latest nightmares," Blake continued. "I think there's one left over from last week, and I had a particularly bad one yesterday. I was walking on the beach at night with Roger. There was a bright moon, so we could see pretty well. There was a big clump of seaweed near the high tide line and we walked over to it. I kicked it, and an arm appeared. Roger pushed away more of the weed, and then we could see it was a woman's dead body. She had long blonde hair and most of her face was gone, obviously eaten by fishes. It was hideous, and I started to scream. That was when I woke up. Of all the nightmares I've had, this was the worst."

"It sounds horrible. How old were you in the dream?"

"I was a kid. Maybe ten or twelve, so Roger would have been in college. I think being a kid made it even more scary. Roger was curious. I would have run once I saw the arm. I wouldn't have gone poking around to see what else was there."

"Did you and Roger say anything to one another in the dream?"

"We hardly ever had conversations in real life, so why would we in a dream?"

"Perhaps, in your dream, you might have wanted to say something to him you couldn't say in real life."

"Such as, you fucker, you killed my cat?"

"Maybe."

"I'll keep it in mind for my next nightmare."

"I want to hear more about your cat," Andrea said. She had a sudden, horrible vision of Molly's kitten, drowned and floating. She shook it off and tried to concentrate.

"I was seven at the time. I came home from school on a hot September day, changed into my bathing suit, and went down for a swim. Sylvester was floating at the deep end, so I yelled for the housekeeper."

"I thought you would have yelled for your mother," Andrea suggested.

"Mother wasn't home. Even if she had been, she'd have just ordered the housekeeper to get the dead cat out of the pool. Mother switched housekeepers as often as she switched outfits. This one was particularly nice, much nicer than my parents. Her name was Ellie. She hugged me. Then she fished Sylvester out of the pool and put him in a plastic bag. She and I buried him together, in a corner of the back yard. Roger watched us with a smug smile on his face. I've never forgotten it. I knew he was responsible."

"In your dream, even though the face on the body wasn't recognizable, could you identify the woman?"

Blake shook his head. "I wondered how she'd gotten there. I imagined she went swimming and got caught in a current she couldn't handle, or maybe she fell overboard from a boat."

Andrea glanced at her notes. "You had a dream where you were on a boat, in a storm, and holding on because you were afraid you'd be dragged overboard."

"It was my Dad's boat, The Joyce. He named it after my mother. It was very posh. He would take us all out on it during the summer, and hold parties on it for his business associates. Doc, do you have any theories about what these dreams could mean?"

"I can think of some possibilities, but you're the one who will have to evaluate them and see if they make any sense to you. I wondered, after you told me about your first two dreams, whether you were afraid of water, but you denied that vehemently. It would have been very difficult for you to scuba dive and be on a swim team if you were."

"Full disclosure, Doc. I wasn't on a team and I don't dive.

I avoid water sports. I lied to you. I think I wanted to impress you."

"Your professional accomplishments are impressive enough, Blake. You didn't have to add anything."

So, he'd lied about that. She wondered what else was a lie.

"I don't like to show any kind of weakness. I guess it comes from being the boss. If there's a crack in your armor, someone will attack."

"Therapists don't attack. This is a safe place to say anything you want to say. I do have another thought," Andrea continued, "now that I know the boat belonged to your family. The boat could be a symbol for your family, and the dream a reflection of your relationship with them."

"You think I was battling to keep my family from drowning me?" he said.

"That's one possibility. Perhaps you were also fighting to stay connected, despite feeling that they were drowning you. Our feelings, especially about our parents, can be pretty conflicted. I'm afraid we are out of time for today. Let's continue this conversation during your next appointment, which will be in two weeks. My office will be closed over the four-day Thanksgiving weekend."

CHAPTER FIFTEEN

IT WAS SATURDAY NIGHT AND BLAKE WAS feeling frustrated and angry. He needed to get laid, but it was unlikely he could hook up with anyone tonight using an app. Fortunately, there were a number of bar scenes in Westwood that attracted co-eds. He dressed in black, combed his hair, and headed out. Maybe he could pick up a woman who looked like Andrea, and who shared his sexual tastes.

His favorite rooftop bar was crowded and noisy, as usual. He elbowed his way to the counter and ordered a craft beer, scanning the room for a likely prospect. There was a woman sitting at the end of the bar, nursing a martini. Her profile didn't look anything like Andrea's, but the body type and the long, honey-colored hair were similar. He liked her short, clinging black dress and her stiletto heels. In addition, she looked a bit older than the college co-eds, whose conversation he always found puerile. He carried his drink in her direction and stood next to her.

"Can I buy you a refill?"

She turned and glanced at him, then smiled. Apparently, she'd decided she liked his looks.

"Maybe a little later. I haven't finished this one."

He smiled back. "I'm Blake."

"Nancy."

"What do you do, Nancy?"

"I'm a UCLA graduate student in psychology," she said.

"Clinical or experimental?" Blake asked.

"Clinical."

How perfect. The closest he was likely to get to a shrink tonight.

"What about you?" she asked.

"I'm a biologist. I work for a pharmaceutical start-up company."

She seemed impressed, and proceeded to ask some moderately intelligent questions. He reciprocated, and for several minutes they had a conversation that was a significant improvement over the usual first date inanities. When they'd both finished their drinks, Blake suggested they go somewhere for a snack. The transition to his apartment was seamless.

"Wow, this is gorgeous!" Nancy looked wide-eyed around his living room at the glittering city view from the floor-to-ceiling penthouse windows. He opened the door to the balcony and took her outside, standing behind her as she leaned on the railing and appreciated the panorama. He pressed against her, running his hands over her breasts and ass. From behind, he could pretend she was Andrea, and that thought excited him.

He turned her around, kissed her, and guided her into his bedroom. Luckily, his housekeeper had been there that morning and his king-sized bed was made, and all his clothes had been laundered and put away. Blake was meticulous about his science but couldn't care less about his home surroundings. He'd hired a decorator to create an acceptable CEO apartment, in case he had to entertain a business client. A bonus was that the décor usually impressed women as well.

He unzipped and undressed her efficiently, and then removed his own clothes. He could tell she admired his body, and hers wasn't bad, although he suspected Andrea's would be better. Reaching for her, he rotated her around and pushed her onto his bed, on her stomach. He grasped both her wrists in his left hand, holding her arms above her head and preventing her from turning over. Then he began to spank her.

"Stop," she yelled. "I don't like that."

"I don't recall asking you what you like." He hit harder. It turned him on to see the red flush on her ass as he slapped.

"I said NO," she shouted.

"You're naked in my apartment. That means you said YES." He pushed her legs apart with his knees. She kicked and fought, but he was on top and stronger. The harder she fought, the more aroused he was. By the time he entered her, he was so turned on, he came in seconds. Letting go and rolling over, he caught his breath.

The moment he released her, she grabbed her dress, her shoes and her purse, and ran for the front door. He hoped she managed to get dressed before someone came up in the elevator. He picked up her lacy bra and bikini panties from the floor, inhaled her scent, and put them in a drawer which included other pieces of lingerie from his liaisons.

Blake walked into the living room, poured himself an inch of single malt Scotch, and sat down in his favorite chair. Maybe tonight, instead of a nightmare, he could relive this evening in his dreams, with Andrea in his bed.

CHAPTER SIXTEEN

BLAKE SAT IN HIS CAR ON SATURDAY MORNING at 7:45 a.m. The car was parked diagonally across the street from Andrea's house, behind a white SUV with a residential parking permit. He'd dreamt about her last night. She was in his apartment, wrists and ankles tied up on his bed, wearing one of her elegant pant suits. He was removing her slacks with a pair of scissors, one leg at a time, exposing her creamy thighs. She was wearing black lace bikini panties and he cut through them. She was crying and begging him to stop, which just aroused him more. Glancing down, he removed his belt, and began to whip her. The louder she screamed, the more excited he became, until he lost control and woke to an intense orgasm and ejaculation. Jesus. If she could do this to him in his sleep, imagine what it would be like for real. Not for the first time, he wondered why it always took pain to arouse him.

The garage door of her home opened and the Porsche Panamera appeared. He let it drive half a block, and then began to follow. The car turned right on Wilshire, left on Sepulveda, and turned into the parking lot of Equinox. How fortunate. She went to his gym. Why had he never noticed her there before?

He waited a few minutes, took his gym bag from the trunk of his car, and presented his membership card at the desk. After changing in the elegantly appointed locker room, he began his search for Andrea on the cardio floor. As he glanced down the aisles, he noticed her working out on an elliptical. She was wearing teal blue yoga pants, which clung to her figure, and a matching tight, sleeveless top. Her arms were firm and well-toned. He chose a machine at the other end of the row behind her, so he could watch her without being noticed.

Twenty minutes later, she slowed down, wiped her forehead and neck with a towel, took a drink from her water bottle, and relocated to a treadmill. Blake followed, once again choosing a machine that was close enough to look, but behind her. After another twenty minutes, he decided that his best chance of accidentally running into her was at the café, which everyone passed on their way out.

He sat at the counter, ordered a protein smoothie with spinach and kale, and sipped slowly, waiting for her to emerge.

"Dr. Marcus," he smiled and waved as she approached. "I didn't know you worked out at my gym. I've never seen you here before."

"I just joined recently," she said. "It's pretty busy here Sunday mornings."

Her face was flushed and tendrils of damp hair curled around her forehead.

"You look like you could use a cool drink," he said. "Please, let me get one for you. What would you like?"

She slid onto the stool next to him and gave her order to the waiter. "Pomegranate juice please, with plenty of ice."

She took the glass and pressed it against her warm cheeks, then drew a long sip through the straw.

"Thanks, Blake. That's thoughtful of you. Do you work out here regularly?"

"Mostly weekends. During the week, I have a private trainer come to my apartment early in the morning. I'm quite religious about my exercise."

She glanced at his green smoothie.

Was that a glimmer of distaste on her lush mouth?

"You certainly seem to lead a healthy lifestyle." Her cell phone rang as she sipped her juice. "Hi. I'll be home in a few minutes. Just getting a quick drink."

Probably her husband, Blake thought. She didn't sound very affectionate.

"Got to go," she said. "Thanks for the juice."

CHAPTER SEVENTEEN

"Damn it," Andrea said, as she walked into the kitchen.

Jonathan looked up from the Sunday New York Times. "What's wrong?"

"I ran in to my least favorite patient at the gym this morning. I feel like I'm being stalked. I've seen him at Whole Foods as well, on Saturday mornings."

"Couldn't that just be a coincidence? You told me he lived in Westwood. Lots of people belong to Equinox."

"I don't think it was a coincidence. He was on the elliptical when I was, and then followed me to the treadmill. I saw him in the mirror. He left before I finished, and then pretended to run into me at the café, as I passed by. He insisted on buying me a cold drink. I couldn't turn him down without being extremely rude."

"You've run into patients before around town. I've never seen you upset about it before."

"I never thought those encounters were anything but accidental."

"How would he know you joined that gym, or what time you would be there?"

Andrea poured herself a mug of coffee and sat down at the kitchen table. "I don't know, unless he's been following me. I need to figure out when I can exercise without running into him."

"Take a Pilates class," Jonathan suggested, reaching over to hold her hand. "It's a girl thing. He'd stick out like a sore thumb doing Pilates."

Andrea laughed. "I'm so glad this week is Thanksgiving. I won't have to see him."

CHAPTER EIGHTEEN

M ONDAY MORNING, BLAKE PERUSED THE NOTES he'd taken the previous week. There was a well-respected prostate cancer oncologist at UCLA, one at USC, and Frank Sanderson at Memorial. He'd start there, in Jonathan Marcus' medical group. He imagined any clinician would be tempted to participate in his ground-breaking research. Humming to himself, he picked up the phone.

"Doctor Sanderson will be with you in a few minutes, Doctor Harris." the smiling receptionist said. Blake took a seat and glanced at his watch. It was almost noon, time for the lunch conference he'd scheduled.

The waiting room was elegant and soothing. A large, scented flower arrangement sat on a glass coffee table, with high end magazines. The chairs were comfortable and upholstered in a palette of pastels taken from the Oriental rug in the center: peach, pale blue, soft gray. The artwork was soothing. The room was designed to calm anxious cancer patients. Blake approved.

"Dr. Harris?" A man in a neatly pressed white coat entered the waiting room and offered his hand. "Pleased to meet you. I'm Frank Sanderson."

Blake stood and shook hands. Sanderson was about forty with a round face, black-framed glasses, a balding head and a well-fed figure. Sanderson opened the door and ushered Blake into the interior of the office.

"I've ordered lunch in, so we can talk undisturbed in the conference room. ," Sanderson said. "I hope that's okay with you. I only have an hour."

"Of course."

"We can get coffee or soft drinks in the kitchen." Sanderson led him down a corridor to a well appointed staff eating space. There was a dark-haired, handsome man seated at one of the lunch tables, chewing on a sandwich.

"Jonathan, meet Dr. Blake Harris of Chess Pharmaceuticals. He's here to tell me about his new prostate cancer drug. Dr. Harris, this is one of my partners, Dr. Jonathan Marcus."

The man rose and shook hands. He was taller than Blake, and had a calm, self-assured demeanor. So, this was the husband. Not bad looking. He wondered how long Andrea had been married to him, and if he was any good in bed.

"Pleased to meet you. Are you also a prostate cancer expert?"

"Not at all. My expertise is in blood cancers."

Sanderson opened the refrigerator and helped himself to a can of Coke. "Would you like a soft drink, or do you prefer tea or coffee?"

"Sparkling water, if you have it."

Sanderson handed him a bottle of Perrier. "The conference room is down the hall," Sanderson said.

Blake followed him out the door, glancing back to see Jonathan Marcus watching them.

There was a platter of sandwiches on the conference room table: roast beef, corned beef, turkey, and luckily, a veggie-wrap. Blake helped himself. Sanderson chose the corned beef. The scent was unpleasant, but Blake ignored it. Opening his briefcase, he removed his data, and began his pitch for a research collaborator.

CHAPTER NINETEEN

"HI, LOVE." ANDREA WAS AT THE KITCHEN SINK, peeling yams, when Jonathan arrived home.

"What are you making?"

"We're going to Hannah and Daniel's for Thanksgiving. I'm in charge of the sweet potato pie." She chopped the yams into large chunks, before immersing them into a pot of boiling water.

"What's going on with them?" Jonathan asked. "You said the honeymoon didn't go as expected. Is there trouble in paradise?"

"They spent their honeymoon solving yet another murder, and then Hannah had a miscarriage. She's pretty depressed." Andrea withheld the part about Daniel's illegitimate son. That was confidential.

"I'm sorry. They seemed so happy at the wedding."

"They were. I'm hoping they'll get past this."

"I had a disconcerting experience at the office today," Jonathan took a seat at the kitchen counter. "I met a man who I suspect is your patient."

"Someone who came in with cancer?" Andrea asked.

"No. Blake Harris, a pharmaceutical researcher who was meeting with Frank to talk to him about his new prostate cancer drug.

"Damn it." Andrea decapitated a yam with a violent stroke. "Blake Harris acted very impressed at my knowledge of immunotherapy. He probably put the pieces together when he saw your name on your group's website, and connected the dots. But what was he doing on your website?"

"I suspect he was researching prostate cancer specialists. According to Frank, he's starting human trials."

"Great. I've been avoiding his personal questions, so now he's prying into my private life from a different direction. Has he tried to become your best friend yet?" Andrea asked.

"No, but I wouldn't be surprised if he's cultivating Frank for more than one reason. Frank is a very nice guy, but he's something of a gossip. A perfect target for someone looking for personal information about us," Jonathan said.

"Frank's not one of our friends or part of our social circle. How much could he know?"

Jonathan shook his head. "I have no idea, but it worries me.

He went to the refrigerator and poured them both a generous glass of white wine. They sat there together, sipping slowly, trying to figure out what Blake Harris was up to, and how Andrea could deal with it.

CHAPTER TWENTY

"H I, Aunt Andrea." Zoe opened the front door and greeted them with a broad smile. She looked adorable in a royal blue velvet dress and a bow in her dark hair. Andrea wondered if Hannah had to bribe her to wear something other than her favorite jeans.

"Hello, pumpkin," Andrea bent down to give her a kiss. "You look very grown up."

"Please, come in," Zoe said. "Everyone's in the den."

"I just need to deliver my sweet potatoes."

Jonathan took Molly by the hand, and headed for the sound of conversation in the den. Zoe followed Andrea to the kitchen.

"Can I talk to you alone?" Zoe whispered.

"Of course, sweetheart. Just let me pop this casserole into the warming oven."

Hannah was in the kitchen, basting the turkey. Emilia, their housekeeper, was tossing a salad. Hannah looked more like herself today. She was wearing wide-legged black slacks and an emerald green sweater that emphasized her eyes.

Her hair was done up in an elegant twist and her face was subtly made up.

Andrea waited until she'd closed the oven, and then hugged her. "It smells fabulous in here."

Hannah smiled, taking the dish from Andrea's hands. "Do go have a drink and some appetizers in the den. Dinner should be ready in about half an hour."

Zoe took Andrea by the hand and led her out. "Come to my room."

Zoe's bedroom was unusually neat for a six-year-old. Andrea sat on the bed and waited.

"I'm worried about Mommy and Daddy." Tears were beginning to form in Zoe's brown eyes.

Andrea opened her arms and Zoe leaned in for a hug. "Tell me what's bothering you."

"Mommy seems so sad all the time. I found her crying the other day, and she and Daddy used to hug all the time, and now they don't. I know something is wrong."

"Did you ask Mommy what was making her unhappy?" Andrea asked.

"I did, and she said she just had a bad day at work, but I don't believe her. I think something else is happening and she isn't telling me. Do you know what's wrong?"

"Would you like me to talk to your Mom and see what I can do?"

Zoe nodded, pressing her head onto Andrea's shoulder.

"You know, sweetheart, sometimes bad things happen in the grown-up world, and we don't tell our children because we don't want them to worry. We try to solve problems ourselves, without upsetting anyone else. Sometimes, if we have trouble hiding our feelings, our children notice and get upset anyway. Often the truth is much better than the bad things we imagine. I'm glad you told me how you feel. How about we go have some appetizers and I'll find time to talk to your mother?"

Zoe pulled away and nodded. Andrea took a tissue from the bedside table, wiped the tears from her cheeks, and the two of them headed for the den.

Molly made a beeline for Zoe as soon as she walked in, and pulled her over to join two other children, belonging to Hannah's medical partner Ruth, and her husband, Arthur. Arthur was a superb chef, who was everyone's favorite dinner guest. Daniel was at the bar, mixing cocktails and chatting with Jonathan. Andrea thought Daniel looked a little haggard.

The other two guests were Daniel's detective partner, Brenda, and her girlfriend, Marcy. Marcy was sipping what looked like a pomegranate martini.

"Daddy, can I have one of those red drinks?" Zoe asked.

Daniel grinned, grabbed a glass and mixed up pomegranate juice, a twist of lime, a spritz of fizzy water, and handed it to her.

"Don't get too drunk."

Zoe smiled back at him and retreated to the children's corner.

A few minutes later, Hannah announced that dinner was served, and everyone helped themselves to the lavish buffet spread.

When she was too full to eat another thing, Andrea helped Hannah and Emilia clear the table for dessert.

"Hannah, I need a few minutes of your time, in private," Andrea said, when they were both in the kitchen.

"Now?"

"Now would be good. Can we go into your study?"

Hannah looked puzzled, but led the way. "What's wrong?"

Andrea sat down next to her friend on the sofa. "What's wrong is that Zoe is worried. She's noticed how depressed you are, and that you and Daniel aren't hugging anymore, and she thinks something bad is happening. She saw you crying and didn't believe it was just a bad day at work. You have a very sensitive and mature little girl."

"I guess I haven't been hiding it very well," Hannah said.

"I realize you don't want to burden her with your feelings about the miscarriage, but she's worried about your relationship with Daniel."

"He's pretty depressed too," Hannah admitted. "We did talk about it, a week ago. I took your advice and told him how I truly felt about what happened with Melanie, and about the miscarriage."

"And?"

"I agreed to the contact he wanted with Josh, assuming he can get Melanie on board, and we both agreed not to make any decisions now about future pregnancies."

"Did you raise the issue of Daniel's infidelity to his first wife?"

"I did. He said he felt terribly guilty afterwards and would never do that to me. He also said he knew he'd have to earn my trust again. That's where we left it."

"Are you feeling any better?"

Hannah shook her head. "I don't know, Andrea. I still feel conflicted. I'm trying to just live our life right now and see what happens."

"I think you and Daniel might need help. The best way to communicate about all these issues is in couple's therapy, if he's willing. Otherwise, you should consider individual therapy, to help sort out your feelings, and decide what you want to do. I can suggest a few names, people I trained with and trust."

Hannah was silent for awhile, staring at her hands, twisting in her lap.

Finally, she looked up. "I have no doubt Daniel would agree to therapy. He's as unhappy as I am. I'll take those names. I'm just unsure that, between our jobs and family, we could find time to do it."

"I'll text them to you when we get home. You might consider telling Zoe about the miscarriage. She's probably imagining things that are much worse, and I think she could handle it."

Hannah reached out, took Andrea's hands and squeezed them. "I'm so glad I have you for a friend."

CHAPTER TWENTY-ONE

"YOUR BROTHER IS WAITING." GEORGE POKED his head into Blake's office. "Here are the consent forms you wanted. Our attorney emailed them this morning."

"Thanks. Show him in, will you?"

A few minutes later, there was a creaking sound in the hallway, and the door opened. A health aide, dressed in green scrubs, pushed Roger, in a wheelchair, through the office door.

Blake was startled. It had been less than three months since he'd seen his brother and the change was striking. He'd lost a large amount of weight. His face was wrinkled. His jowls hung, and his complexion was yellowed. Blake suspected the tumor had infiltrated the liver. He was wearing a short-sleeved, paisley sport shirt, and when Roger reached out to shake Blake's hand, Blake noticed his brother's triceps flapping like a bat wing. Treating his cancer was going to be even more of a challenge than Blake had anticipated.

Roger turned toward his aide. "You can wait for me in the lobby," he said. "I'll call when I'm ready to leave."

"I didn't realize things had progressed so far," Blake said.

"My PSA level resembled the Dow Jones Industrial Average last week," Roger said. "If your drug cures me, it can cure anyone. Thanks, by the way, little brother."

Blake couldn't remember if Roger had ever thanked him for anything. He relished the reversal of their fortunes.

"I got permission from the FDA," he said, "and I've found you an oncologist in the best group at Memorial Hospital. He'll be handling your infusions, and has arranged for you to have baseline scans and blood tests tomorrow. All that remains is for you to sign the consent form."

He handed Roger several pages of detailed description of the treatment, potential side effects, including death, and an agreement binding him and his estate not to sue for any negative outcome. Roger flipped to the last page, signed it and handed it back.

"Aren't you going to read it?" Blake asked.

"I'm hardly in a negotiating position. I'll do whatever it takes to get your drug."

Blake handed him another piece of paper. "Show up at the oncology office tomorrow morning at 9:00 a.m. I assume you can be reached on your cell phone?"

"Of course. And I'll be at the Beverly Hills Hotel, if you need to reach me on a landline."

"Did you tell the parents you were in town?"

"I'll tell them if your treatment works. Otherwise, you can have the pleasure of notifying them to plan my funeral."

"No reason to be snarky," Blake said. "But I do hope your estate plan is current."

~

Blake decided to be at the oncologist's on Thursday morning, when Roger had his first infusion. He'd spoken to Sanderson when the test results came back.

"Your brother has widespread disease in his spine, long bones and skull, and a few small lesions in his liver. We'll be following his symptoms and chemistries frequently because, as you know, immune therapy drugs can have fatal complications. Yours may be a stronger drug than most. I'm planning to begin with a very small dose and go up slowly."

Blake was glad that the Memorial Cancer group had its own chemotherapy center, so they didn't have to wade through red tape to medicate Roger at the hospital-based one. The center was on the second floor of their office building.

"I'm sending private duty nurses to the hotel with him after chemotherapy, to monitor his vital signs and check for a list of symptoms," Sanderson added.

"You're the clinical boss," Blake said. "We'll do it however you think best."

The Chemotherapy Center consisted of a large nursing station, surrounded by small cubicles, each of which had a hospital bed, a chair, and an attached utilitarian sink and toilet. Roger was propped up in the bed, attached to an IV and an infusion pump.

"Nervous, brother?" Blake asked, as he walked into the room.

"Trying to be optimistic," Roger said. "Did you come to preside over your investment?"

"Exactly. I'm rooting for you to live. If you do, it's a win for me. Did you tell your wife you were doing this?"

"Yeah. She had no interest in keeping me company. She's not the caregiver type."

"You mean she'd rather inherit your purse, than be your nurse?"

"Very funny." Roger glared at him. "Gloria's gorgeous and a great lay. I didn't marry her for her skill with bedpans. When was the last time you got laid, little brother?"

"Speaking of getting laid, I had an interesting dream about you. You and a few buddies were gang-raping a woman. It was quite exciting."

"Pleased to know that my sex life turns you on."

"Have you ever actually raped someone?" Blake asked.

"Just once. A few of us were very drunk. It was at a pool party at our house, Labor Day weekend, my senior year. The parents were out of town and I was babysitting you."

"Where was I when all this excitement was going on?"

"Asleep, I assume. It was pretty late."

Blake had a sudden vision of Roger telling him to go to bed, and of sneaking into the pool house instead.

"Did she report you to the police?"

A strange expression crossed Roger's face, and then disappeared. "I don't think so. The police never questioned any of us. She was pretty wasted at the time."

Just then, Dr. Sanderson came in, followed by a nurse carrying a tray with a small IV bag, which she hung.

"This is your pre-medication for nausea. As soon as it's gone in, we'll begin the immune therapy."

"I'll get out of your way," Blake said. "Good luck, bro."

As Blake walked down the hall, he found himself short of breath. His pulse was racing. The last time he'd been this nervous was just before his PhD oral examination. He took a few deep breaths and counted to ten, trying to calm himself. Intense memories were coming back. That dream did represent a reality he had repressed. In addition, his future business was at stake, depending on whether Roger responded to the therapy or died, and there was nothing he could do to affect the outcome.

As soon as he reached his office, he stopped at the lab to check with George on the latest experiments.

"How are my rats today?" Blake looked in each of the multiple cages. The lab always had an unpleasant smell, despite the lab techs efforts to keep the cages clean. He thought the scent had something to do with the many growing tumors with which the animals had been inoculated. He was pleased to note that the cancers had grown rapidly.

"Looks like we might be ready to start treatment on a few of these."

"The pancreatic and colon cancer group are growing nicely. I'll be able to begin giving them the drug tomorrow. The sarcomas aren't ready yet. Maybe next week," George said.

"Wouldn't it be a coup if we got remissions for these as well?" Blake said.

"Once we're done with these experiments, we really should meet with some of the big drug companies."

"Have you contacted the venture capitalists?"

"I'm waiting on our results. If the drug works on more than just prostate cancer, we'll be in a much stronger position to attract major investors."

"If our results are that good, Blakimab will be worth billions," Blake said.

"And if it doesn't work on any other cancers?" George asked.

"No need to even mention that we've tried. In any case, we need to see how our human trial works out. I'll be in my office. Don't disturb me unless it's critical."

Blake closed his office door, made himself a cup of chamomile tea, and sat down at his computer. He started to work on a journal article, but couldn't concentrate. Opening his browser, he went to Truthfinder.com, a useful website that collected reams of data on anyone you wanted to look up. You had to pay, of course, for the good stuff, but it wasn't very expensive and they did a comprehensive search of multiple databases. He always insisted that his human resources department use it to check out prospective employees prior to hiring.

He typed in "Andrea Marcus, MD" and hit enter. Then he waited while the computer searched educational, real estate, legal and crime databases for information. He'd been meaning to do this for weeks. He printed out his findings and looked them over. A smile crossed his face. He knew exactly what he wanted to do next, and he was looking forward to telling her his recently recovered memories.

CHAPTER TWENTY-TWO

"Happy birthday, Mommy." Molly took a leap and landed on top of Andrea in the parental king-sized bed.

"Thank you, love," Andrea said. She kissed her daughter and relocated her. "What time is it?"

"It's almost seven-thirty," Jonathan said, rolling over.

"Daddy and I could bring you breakfast in bed," Molly suggested.

"That's a wonderful idea. I'd love it, but can we do it tomorrow? You and I have to get dressed, so you can go to nursery school and I won't be late for work. Tomorrow is Saturday."

"Okay, Mommy, we'll do it tomorrow. Daddy and I are taking you to dinner tonight."

"Really? Where are we going?"

"Molly and I haven't decided yet between Denny's and McDonald's," Jonathan said.

Andrea made a face at him and climbed out of bed.

"Go put some clothes on," she said to Molly, who obediently left the room.

"Happy birthday, darling," Jonathan took her into his arms. "You look very sexy for an old woman of thirty-three."

He slipped his hands underneath her nightgown and drew her closer for a kiss.

"To be continued tonight," she said, slipping out of his arms. "Would you care to join me in the shower?"

"I thought you'd never ask."

By the time Andrea reached her office it was ten minutes to nine. When she entered the waiting room, she noticed a large ceramic plant container on the coffee table, filled with at least a half dozen orchids. It was gorgeous.

"Where did this come from?" she asked Charles, who was helping himself to a cup of coffee in the utility room.

"It arrived early this morning for you. I think there's a card."

There was a card:

Happy Birthday, signed with a smiley face.

"Who's it from?" Charles asked.

"It doesn't say, but probably Jonathan. I don't advertise my birthday and Molly isn't old enough for her own credit card."

She pulled out her phone as she entered her consult room and sent off a quick text to Jonathan:

Thanks, darling. They're lovely.

Then she prepared herself for her nine o'clock patient.

During her ten minute break she checked her phone for texts.

I'd love to claim credit, but I didn't send you anything.
You have to wait until tonight.

Andrea had a bad feeling. Someone else had sent her the anonymous gift and she had a hunch she knew who it was.

～

She found Blake sprawled on the sofa in the waiting room, reading a magazine.

"Hi, Doc. Nice flower arrangement."

"Yes, it is. Several of my patients have commented on it. Would you like to come in?"

He followed her into her consult room. Andrea waited to see if he would say anything more about the flowers. She was sure, from the smug expression on his face, that he was responsible.

"I enjoyed seeing you at the gym over the weekend. It's nice to know you have a life outside the office."

"Like most people, I shop for groceries and try to get some exercise. I hope you enjoyed your Thanksgiving weekend."

"I missed you, Doc. Two weeks is a long time. You'll be pleased to hear that Roger began his immune therapy trial yesterday. I even went over there to see him get started."

"How is he doing?" Andrea asked.

"No major side effects so far. Just a little diarrhea. They'll be increasing the dose next week."

"When will you know if it's working?"

"They'll be drawing his PSA, his prostate-specific antigen blood test, at the end of his second infusion and following it every week. As long as it keeps going down, the therapy is working. I imagine they'll do a scan at some point, to measure the size of his tumors and compare them to baseline."

"Well, for both your sakes, I hope the trial is a success. How are you feeling?"

"Hungry. I missed breakfast."

"I can offer you some coffee, but none of the snacks I keep in the office are vegan."

"I have an idea," Blake said. "Why don't I take you out to lunch? We can have our session over a nice meal. My treat."

"I'm afraid not. I don't go to lunch with my patients. It's a boundary issue. Happy to bring you coffee, though. I assume you take it black."

Was he ever going to stop pushing those boundaries?

"You assume correctly."

She stepped out of her office for a minute and returned with a mug of steaming coffee. She found him standing close to her desk. Had he been snooping? If so, he would be disappointed. He took the coffee from her and reseated himself.

"I suppose you'd like to hear another nightmare," he said.

"If you've had one."

Andrea remained expressionless.

Blake continued. "This dream was interesting. I was on a roof, with a pair of night vision binoculars. The street below me was dark and deserted. Then a girl appeared, walking. She had long blonde hair, and was wearing a short dress and high heels. She was hurrying as if she was afraid, and clutching her purse to her chest. Four guys stepped out of an alley and surrounded her. She started to scream, but one of them grabbed her from behind and covered her mouth. Two others grabbed her legs and pulled them apart, and the last guy tore off her panties and started raping her. Then, they changed places. It was like a dance, each of them rotating clockwise while she struggled. Then there was a clap of thunder and it started to rain very heavily, so I couldn't see any more."

A shiver passed over Andrea's body and she dug her fingers into the arms of her chair. "This dream seems different. In all your other dreams, except the very first one, you were frightened. You described this one as interesting."

"I get what you're suggesting."

"Did you recognize any of the men, or the woman who was raped?"

"One of the men was Roger. I didn't recognize anyone else. When I was a kid, I used to spy on him. We had two bedrooms with a bathroom between them. Sometimes, when he had one of his girlfriends in his room, I'd tiptoe into the bathroom and crack the door enough to see. He was sufficiently occupied not to notice. That's how I learned about sex."

"Have you ever dreamed about committing a rape yourself?" Andrea stared over his shoulder, not meeting his eyes.

"Sometimes. But why don't you ask what you really want to know? Whether or not I've ever raped someone. The answer is that I don't have to resort to rape to have sex. It's not difficult, in the internet world, to find willing partners."

"I see."

"I had another dream about that woman, the dead one on the beach. This time, I came home to my apartment and smelled something fishy. When I walked into my bedroom, she was lying naked on my bed, dead and covered with seaweed. That woke me up pretty quickly."

"I can imagine it was horrifying. Do you mind if I ask you if you've recently had any sexual contact? I know you said you didn't have time for a relationship, but that doesn't rule out casual sex."

"No, Doc, I don't mind. I'm happy to tell you about my

sex life. You might find it interesting." He gave her his most disarming smile.

Andrea was beginning to regret asking that question. Blake looked all too eager to regale her with his sexual exploits.

"I never dated in high school. I was a nerd and girls don't pay attention to nerds. I didn't date until I started MIT."

Andrea imagined there were any number of smart scientists at MIT, possibly the best place for Blake to have found someone who interested him.

"In my day, there weren't many women at MIT, and I always thought it would be awkward to have a bad date with someone I saw every day in Physics class, so I hunted elsewhere. Boston is full of college girls. This was before Facebook, or online dating, but there were plenty of mixers and bars. It was easy to meet girls and date casually."

"So, even then, you weren't interested in a long term relationship."

"No. I didn't want to have to consider anyone else when I made future plans. To answer your original question, I did pick up a woman at a bar, the weekend before Thanksgiving. I should probably tell you about my sexual tastes. I find that I'm most aroused by acting out sexual fantasies. Sometimes, those fantasies involve a little light bondage."

Andrea struggled to keep a non-judgmental expression on her face.

"Bondage involves psychological as well as physical dominance," Blake continued. "With an experienced partner, you create a scenario, choose parts and play them."

"Does it ever get violent?"

"There's a safe word. The non-dominant partner can always stop the action."

"Provided she trusts the person she's with."

Blake smiled again. "There is that."

Andrea suspected that light bondage was a euphemism. "Tell me what you think the connection is between your sexual tastes and your dream."

"Maybe the dream was a warning not to go too far."

"Or not to lose control during a sexual encounter," Andrea said.

"I never lose control. I'm always careful. Unfortunately, the woman I picked up wasn't into it. She actually ran out of my apartment. All I did was start to spank her." He shrugged and changed the subject. "I had a very interesting conversation with my brother when I went to see him on Thursday."

Andrea waited for him to continue.

"I told him about my rape dream, and then I asked him if he'd ever raped anyone."

Andrea inhaled a sharp breath. "And, had he?"

"He had. He told me all about it."

Andrea wasn't sure if she could stand listening to any more detail.

Blake leaned back looking supremely satisfied.

The silence between them deepened.

"I think I may understand the connection between my dreams and water. Roger and his fraternity buddies gang-raped a girl at our house, during a pool party."

"Is that what he told you?"

"He told me, and I remembered. I must have been twelve at the time. He was home from college for the summer, and the parents were away for the Labor Day weekend. Roger was supposed to be in charge, and when his friends came over, he told me to go to bed. Of course, I didn't. I never obeyed Roger. I snuck into the pool house, took a beer from the refrigerator, and spied on them. I saw the rape."

"How did you react to seeing it?"

"You want the truth?"

"There isn't any point to therapy if you don't tell the truth."

"The truth is that it turned me on. It was exciting. I remember wishing I could get in line and do it too, but I knew Roger would blow a gasket if he saw me spying. Does getting turned on make me a bad person, Doc?"

"You were a twelve-year-old kid. Does the thought of rape still turn you on?"

"Yeah, it does."

Once again, there was a long silence.

Finally, Andrea broke it. She felt as if she was walking on eggshells with him, afraid to say anything that might set off his anger, or inspire him to act on his fantasies about her.

"Tell me what else you remember about that night."

"I don't remember anything else, but I have a feeling that I should. I haven't had a chance to think much about it. I've been pretty absorbed in work."

"Maybe something will come to you before you see me again, next week," Andrea suggested.

"Yeah, maybe." Blake looked at his watch, got up, handed her a check, and headed for the door.

Andrea closed it behind him, leaning against it and shaking. Her intuition, as always, had been right on. She looked carefully at the handwriting on the check, and took the gift card out of her pocket. They were the same. How had he known that today was her birthday?

This guy was scary. She knew he was holding something back, and she was becoming convinced that the dead body in his dream was real. This session had unlocked memories of her own, that she thought she'd forced to the back of her mind, but now, they refused to stay there. They welled up like a geyser, overwhelming her brain.

CHAPTER TWENTY-THREE

AFTER SHE'D SEEN HER LAST PATIENT, ANDREA waited until she heard the outer door shut, and then headed to the kitchen, hoping that Charles might be there. He was.

"Charles. I don't know if I can do this anymore." Tears began to spill down her cheeks.

"Andrea, what is it?"

She accepted his gentle hug. He held her the way her father used to when she was upset, before he'd died of a massive heart attack, a few days after she'd started college.

"This last session with my difficult patient brought out memories for me I thought I'd dealt with years ago and put behind me. Can we talk?"

He pulled a clean handkerchief out of his pocket and tenderly wiped the tears away. Her father had carried a real handkerchief as well. She inhaled the scent of spicy aftershave.

"Of course. Come on. Let's get out of this office and take a walk on campus. We could both use the exercise. We'll find someplace quiet."

The quiet place was a bench in the campus sculpture garden. They had it to themselves this late in the day.

"I've never seen you so upset after a patient session. What happened?"

"He had a dream in which his brother and a few of his brother's buddies gang-raped a woman. I'm convinced the dream is a clue to a bigger story. It really upset me."

"Were you frightened that he might try to assault you?"

"I wouldn't be surprised if he has fantasies about it, but that's not it. It's something else, something I've never told anyone, even Jonathan."

"Would you feel comfortable telling me?"

"Yes." She took a breath. "I was raped in college when I was a freshman. I was still a virgin at the time. It was the worst thing that ever happened to me."

Friday October 13th*, 2000*

"Please come with me, Andrea. You can't spend the entire weekend studying for your Freshman Chemistry exam. Sigma Chi throws great parties."

Andrea looked up from her textbook. Michelle, her roommate, was dressed to kill in a slinky red dress and stiletto heels. As usual, she was smiling and bubbly with warmth and good humor. Andrea had lucked out with her room assignment.

"I'm really not in a party mood tonight," she said. "But I appreciate you asking."

Michelle walked over and put a hand on Andrea's shoulder.

"I know you're still grieving for your Dad, but how do you think he'd feel, knowing his daughter was missing out on the fun part of college. There's more to life than getting straight-A's in all

your Pre-Med classes. Besides, I hate going alone to these things. I need a buddy."

Andrea gave in. This was the first time Michelle had asked Andrea to do anything for her, and she'd been so kind and supportive after Andrea had gotten the awful news from her mother.

"Okay. I guess I have to change."

"Good idea. Those pajamas might give someone the wrong idea."

~

The party was going strong when the two girls arrived. There was loud music, a large crowd, and an ample supply of beer. The sweet scent of marijuana infiltrated the room. Andrea had changed into a black dress and a pair of strappy flat sandals. At least, her feet would be comfortable.

A tall, good-looking frat brother greeted them and pointed them in the direction of the bar. As befit a classy fraternity, a bartender was making mixed drinks. Beer and cheap wine were available for those who wanted to help themselves. Michelle asked for a margarita, and Andrea asked for just the mix. The last thing she felt like doing was getting drunk at a frat party.

She looked around the room and recognized no one. UC San Diego was a big school, and she hadn't been there very long. Everyone seemed very good looking. The fraternity had a reputation for pledging only handsome men, and she suspected that many of the pretty girls were in sororities. Michelle happily worked her way through the room, introducing herself and chatting. Andrea, who hated large parties with strangers, just followed in her wake.

The adjacent room was larger, and had a dance floor in the center and a DJ. Someone asked Michelle to dance and she followed him happily into the crowd of fast moving students.

Andrea leaned against the wall and sipped her drink. The only thing that could make this worse would be disco lights to add a headache to the annoyance of the loud music.

She looked at her watch. It was almost 11:30 p.m. Could she make an exit at midnight and leave Michelle to return to the dorm on her own? It was a short walk and a safe one. Clearly, Michelle was in her element and hadn't really needed Andrea to go with her. She wished, occasionally, that she could be as socially adept as her roommate.

A tall man with a blonde crew cut approached and asked her to dance. She put her empty glass on a table and joined him. As they reached the floor, the music got slower and the lights dimmed. He held her close and she could feel his hand moving from her back to her buttocks. She tried pulling back, but he had her in too tight an embrace. She couldn't wait for the music to be over.

"Can I get you another drink?" he asked.

"No, thanks. I'm just going to run to the ladies," she said.

She felt his eyes on her as she walked to the powder room, only to find it occupied and a woman waiting.

"There's one upstairs, down the hall on your right, if your bladder is too full to wait," the woman said.

Andrea thanked her and climbed the stairs. She took her time in the bathroom, washing her hands, combing her hair and reapplying her lipstick. It was almost midnight. She'd find Michelle and ask if it was okay with her for Andrea to leave. The music was muted up here and she dreaded opening the door. When she did, she found her dance partner waiting for her and blocking her exit.

"Excuse me," she said, trying to duck past him.

He ignored her, pushing her back into the bathroom, and closing the door behind them.

"I wouldn't have taken you for the kind of girl who likes to fuck in the bathroom," he said.

"I'm not. Leave me alone."

"I don't like chicks who lead me on and don't deliver." He shoved her against the wall, covering her mouth with his hand and leaning on her. She tried to bring her knee up to disable him, but it was too late. He was much stronger. He pushed her legs apart and pulled down her panties. Then he forced her to the floor, her head resting on the bathmat, and unzipping his pants, shoved himself inside her.

It hurt like hell. She was sure she was bleeding, and she wanted to scream but his hand was still over her mouth. He pumped up and down, and then let out a groan and pulled out.

"Shit. You got blood on my good slacks." He grabbed a towel and cleaned off his bloody, limp penis. Then he zipped up, threw the towel at her, and left the room.

Andrea moaned, got to her feet and locked the door. Then she sat down on the toilet and cried her heart out.

When she used up all her tears, she found a washcloth and wet it with warm water. She'd had adequate sex education and knew that cleaning up after a rape would destroy evidence, but it didn't matter. She would never go to the police. No one could know about this. It was the most humiliating, devastating thing that had ever happened to her. She washed herself thoroughly and put a dry, folded washcloth between her panties and her bruised genitals, just in case there was more bleeding.

Thank God, her period was due in a day or two. She wouldn't have to worry about pregnancy, but she would have to do something to prevent a sexually transmitted disease.

With her hands still shaking, she straightened her dress, washed her face, and reapplied makeup. She had to look normal when she opened that door.

As she walked downstairs, she spotted Michelle, who waved at her.

"I've been looking for you. Are you okay? Where were you?"

"Bathroom," Andrea said. "Bad period cramps. Can we leave now?"

"Sure. I've already given my number to three very cute guys, so mission accomplished."

Andrea led the way to the front door, and took a deep breath of fresh air as she exited the house. She hadn't spotted her rapist on her way out. It was a big campus. With luck, she'd never see him again.

~

"Andrea, I'm so sorry," Charles said. "No wonder you were in tears earlier. Listening to your patient must have brought all that back in force. Did you report it to the police?"

"This was way before the #MeToo movement. I was humiliated, and I didn't think anyone would believe me. I couldn't even tell my mother. She was still dealing with her grief over my Dad's recent death. I couldn't do anything more to upset her."

"So, you've held this in all these years. Did you ever think of seeing a therapist or a rape counselor?"

"I did the next best thing. I became a therapist and did some training at the rape treatment center at Santa Monica hospital. It was a way to exorcize my demons without admitting to them."

"And Jonathan?"

"I was embarrassed to admit I'd been stupid enough to allow some guy to get the better of me. I didn't want it to interfere with our sexual relationship. It took me several years before I was able to have sex with anyone. Then, I met Jonathan, and he was perfect for me. I couldn't risk telling him, and having him think less of me."

"Andrea, you're talking as if it was your fault. You know

better than that. You're the victim here. If someone robbed you at gunpoint, no one would blame you."

"My head knows that, but my gut isn't listening. I don't know if I can keep treating this guy, and I don't know how to get rid of him without fixing his problem. I'm scared to push him too far. I think he's stalking me. I've run into him several times in Westwood, and he keeps asking me personal questions, and coming on to me."

"Do you think he's a danger?"

"He denied having raped anyone personally, but I don't believe him. I think he is capable of rape. And just because a man can find willing partners, doesn't mean that raping someone doesn't satisfy some twisted part of his psyche."

"It sounds as if you may be describing a psychopath," Charles said.

"I think so, as well. I've never felt frightened of a patient before. "

"I assume you've given some thought to ending his therapy."

Andrea sighed. "I wish I'd never started, but I can't stop now. I'm afraid if I try to refer him to someone else, he'll get angry, and I don't know what he's capable of."

"If it makes you feel safer, I promise not to go out to lunch on Fridays while you are treating him. That way, you will never be alone in the office. I'll leave my door open, so he knows someone else is here."

"Thanks, Charles. That helps."

"Let's head back. It's getting cold." He stood up and offered his arm to her.

She took it. "It's also getting late. I have a dinner date out with my family."

∽

"Molly and I decided that McDonald's wasn't an appropriate birthday place for you," Jonathan said, as they were escorted to their table at Pizzicotto, their favorite, child-friendly Italian restaurant.

"This is perfect," Andrea said.

"What was it you were texting me about?" Jonathan asked.

"Someone sent me flowers this morning, with an anonymous Happy Birthday card. I thought they were from you, but they were from a patient."

Jonathan glanced at Molly and raised his eyebrows. Andrea nodded. Not a conversation for a family dinner. She was still feeling shaky, and not in a birthday mood, but she forced herself to smile. It was bad enough that Blake had ruined her day. She wasn't going to let him ruin Jonathan's or Molly's.

"We have a birthday present for you, Mommy," Molly said. "I helped Daddy pick it out."

She handed Andrea a small package.

Andrea unwrapped it to find a velvet box, in which were a beautiful pair of topaz earrings. "They're gorgeous. You have fabulous taste."

Molly gave her a huge smile.

"She does, actually. I'm not sure I could have picked these out without her."

The waiter delivered two glasses of Chianti and one of Coke.

Molly raised her glass. "Happy Birthday, to our favorite Mommy."

Jonathan leaned over and kissed her. "Happy Birthday, my love."

CHAPTER TWENTY-FOUR

W**HEN BLAKE GOT TO THE OFFICE IN THE** morning, the first thing he did was drop into the lab to check out the rats with colon and pancreatic cancer. George gave him a thumbs up.

"Results?" Blake asked

"It looks like the colon cancer tumors are shrinking. Some of the smallest ones have already disappeared. The pancreatic cancer hasn't responded yet. Those rats may need an increased dose. I'll be starting the sarcoma group on therapy today."

"Good. Even if we only identify two responsive cancers, we'll be in a great position for extra funding. Let's start a breast and ovarian cancer group as well."

"You got it, boss."

"I'll be at my desk if you need me"

Blake closed the door of his private space and put in a call to

Sanderson. He wanted to check on his most important lab rat.

"I was about to call you," Sanderson said. "Your brother's PSA has decreased by fifty percent, after only two infusions."

"That's good news. Any worrisome side effects?"

"So far, just the usual fatigue, nausea and diarrhea. He's a little anemic. I'm holding off on the next treatment for now. We'll follow his PSA daily. As long as it keeps going down, we know his immune system is activated. If his PSA plateaus, I'll give him more drug."

"Why not another dose now?" Blake asked.

"This is a very powerful drug, with which I have no clinical experience. I don't want to risk a full-blown auto immune reaction. I prefer to be cautious, but it looks as if the therapy is working well."

"You've made my day," Blake said.

He should probably plan another visit to Roger, but best to wait until he was feeling better and was convinced he was in remission. Then he'd owe Blake, big time. Blake wondered if Roger had failed to relate the entire story of the rape. Could he have omitted something that Blake didn't remember? If Blake's memory didn't kick in, he would grill his brother.

The house was in the hills, with floor-to-ceiling glass windows that showcased its spectacular view of downtown Los Angeles. Blake couldn't remember who the host was. Waitresses in low-cut, black and white maid's uniforms circulated among the guests, with trays of hors d'oeuvres, and flutes of champagne. Blake helped himself to a drink, and a large shrimp dipped in cocktail sauce. He ambulated through the room, watching the

beautiful people. The women were breathtaking, and clearly paid escorts. Some wore low-cut long gowns, the skirts slit up to their thighs. Others wore bustiers and garter belts with black stockings. Some appeared nude under sheer negligees. Couples groped one another in dark corners, or screwed one another brazenly, on a sofa in the middle of the room. It was truly a bacchanal.

As Blake contemplated choosing a partner for himself, a beautiful blonde approached him and took his hand.

"Come outside," she whispered.

A brunette appeared on his other side, relieved him of his champagne glass, and took his other hand. How nice. A threesome.

Outside was a huge patio with couples copulating on the chaise lounges, and an infinity pool.

"Let us help you with your clothes," the blonde said.

She unbuttoned his shirt and ran her hands over his well-developed pectorals, as the brunette undid his belt and zipper, and stripped him of his pants. He was erect and ready. This was going to be fun. They urged him down on a chaise lounge.

The blonde motioned to several women in the pool, and four of them, all nude and stunning, joined them. One of them grabbed his arms, and tied his hands behind his back. The other three immobilized his legs by tying his ankles. Blake was a little disconcerted. He loved S&M games, but he always got to dominate.

"What's next, ladies?" he asked, hoping his erection would hold up for the games.

"Shut up," the blonde said, sticking a gag into his mouth.

The six of them lifted him up, and swung his body back and forth, as they approached the pool.

They were going to throw him in. He couldn't swim tied up, and he wouldn't be able to breathe. He was going to drown. Blake arched his back and tried to kick, anything to get them to stop, but his efforts were futile. With a final lunge, the women sent his body flying into the deep end of the pool, and he sank.

He held his breath, hoping that when he reached bottom he could push himself up off the concrete, and kick his way to the surface. He tried to spit out the gag. His lungs were burning. With all his force, he propelled himself upward, only to encounter vicious hands, pushing his head under the water once again.

Blake jolted awake, his heart pounding, nauseated and coughing. He ran for the bathroom, retching into the porcelain bowl. This was the most horrifying dream he'd ever had.

It was 2:00 a.m., and he wouldn't get any more sleep tonight Maybe he should quit therapy. Obviously, it had done nothing to solve his problem. On the other hand, he couldn't resist telling her about this dream. He knew it would make her uncomfortable, and he enjoyed watching her try to keep her composure. She was a master at it.

He was getting tired of the slow progress he was making with solving his problem and with coming on to his therapist. No more pomegranate juice for her. No more following her around and accidentally running into her. It was time to be more assertive. Fortunately, his next therapy session was in only ten more hours.

CHAPTER TWENTY-FIVE

B LAKE SAT IN ANDREA'S WAITING ROOM, AN angry expression on his face. She opened the door and he pushed past her, seating himself on the sofa; arms crossed, legs tightly together. She needed to calm him down.

"You look upset," Andrea said.

"Well, I have good news and bad news. Which would you like to hear first?"

"It's always nice to start with good news."

"Roger's cancer is responding well and he's tolerating my drug. I might actually save the bastard's life."

"You don't sound happy about that."

"I am happy, but not for reasons you would approve. We've talked about this before. You know how I feel about my brother."

"I do."

"Let's proceed to the bad news." Blake leaned forward, placing his hands on his knees, glaring at her. "Last night, I had the most horrifying dream I've ever had. I woke up and actually puked, I was so frightened. I thought remembering would eliminate the dreams, not make them worse."

"Can you tell me the dream?"

Blake described it, in all its detail, including everything he thought and felt as it was going on. Andrea didn't take her eyes off him.

"I'm thinking of stopping therapy. Clearly, it's making things worse, not better. I'm exhausted. What do you think about my dream, Doc?"

Andrea took a breath and waited a few seconds before responding. She needed to be very careful.

"I think this dream is telling you that you remembered some part of a trauma, but not all of it. In one of your dreams, you saw Roger and his friends raping a woman, something that actually happened. You remembered seeing it after your conversation with your brother. In this dream, your subconscious started with an erotic fantasy, and then turned the tables and showed you what it felt like to be the victim of a rape. You were out of control and at the mercy of others. You were terrified."

Blake nodded, chewing on his lower lip. "I was. Are you saying I only remembered act one of a two act drama?"

"Possibly. There's a death theme in many of your dreams. Roger drowns in the family pool. You drowned in a pool. You and Roger discover the body of a dead woman on the beach. Her dead body reappears in your bed. You crash your car into the river and can't get out. I suspect that there's more to remember."

"If I quit therapy and stop trying to remember, maybe these dreams will stop."

"Maybe, but you weren't in therapy when they started. It's entirely up to you, Blake. You can only make progress in therapy if you want to be here. I won't try to talk you out of quitting, but there's no guarantee that quitting will make things any better."

Andrea bit her lip to keep herself from saying more.

Blake quitting therapy and getting out of her life would be the answer to her prayers. But it wouldn't be ethical to push him into it, when he so clearly still needed some kind of help. Like it or not, she had to be honest with her assessment.

Blake got up and handed Andrea her check. "I'll leave a message next week and let you know if I'm coming back," he said.

As he walked out, he slammed the door behind him.

Andrea's thoughts were spinning. While part of her hoped that Blake would quit and she could get this hostile, scary patient out of her life, another part was certain she was on the right track, that Blake had witnessed or experienced something horrific.

She was convinced that a gang rape was only part of what happened that night. Could someone have died in that pool? Blake said he was twelve when the rape happened, and his brother was home from college for Labor Day weekend. What if she checked the local Newport Beach newspaper or the Orange County Register for 1981? Maybe there would be a report of a dead body or a missing woman.

She doubted she'd find anything online. She'd have to go to the library and check the microfiche. Of course, she could ask Daniel. He had access to police files. If there was something to be found, he'd be more likely to find it than she would.

No, that was premature. She'd do her homework first. Perhaps she could enlist Hannah's help. If they found something, there was plenty of time to ask Daniel if he could track down details that the reporters might not have had.

As she thought about it, she was surprised to find her

feelings were so ambivalent. The part of her that was Dr. Marcus actually wanted Blake to come back. He was a fascinating professional challenge. But Andrea, the woman, wanted him as far away from her as possible, and was hoping she'd seen the last of him.

CHAPTER TWENTY-SIX

F RIDAY NIGHT, AFTER DINNER, ANDREA CALLED Hannah. "How are you sweetie?"

"Hanging in there," Hannah said. "We're considering your advice."

"I'm glad. I called because I need to do a little sleuthing, and I was wondering if you would like to join me for a girl's day tomorrow. You can practice your well-honed detective skills."

"Is something wrong?"

"I have a patient-related problem. I want to go to the main library downtown, and see if I can find any facts to corroborate something he's told me. I'll tell you what I can on the way there, and I'll treat you to lunch at one of the hot new restaurants."

"You're on. But I'm driving."

Hannah picked Andrea up at her house at 9:00 a.m. on

Saturday morning. Once they got on the freeway, Hannah broke the silence. "So, what are we looking for?"

"I have a difficult patient, whom I believe repressed a childhood memory of seeing a significant crime. His memory is beginning to come back, but he's very manipulative, and I don't trust what he's told me. He's been quite specific about the time and location of the crime, and I want to check the local newspapers to see if I can find any evidence that he's telling the truth."

"What kind of a crime, where and when?" Hannah asked.

"A gang rape, Labor Day weekend, 1981, in Newport Beach. There are two old newspapers called the Newport Beach Times and the Ensign, as well as the Orange County Register, which has a Newport Beach section."

"You do realize that women often don't report their rapes to the police, especially in 1981, when it was usual to blame the victim."

"I know that. But I also suspect that, if he's telling the truth, there may be more to this crime than rape."

"Such as...murder?"

"Maybe. In any case, I thought it might be worth looking for rapes, missing women, and found bodies in the month of September. It's a big job, so I thought it would go twice as fast if we worked together."

Andrea looked at Hannah, whose brows were furrowed in thought. Did she think this was a wild goose chase and a lost cause?

"If there was a rape that weekend, and if we come across a report of a missing woman, we can ask Daniel for help," Hannah suggested. "He can contact the Newport Beach police department and ask to look into old records. If the missing person and the rape are connected, we'll probably find that information within the first couple of weeks in September, depending on when Labor Day fell that year."

~

The Central Library in downtown Los Angeles was a masterpiece of Art Deco architecture originally built in 1926 and renovated and expanded in the 1990s. Made of buff-colored stone, decorated with impressive sculpture, it possessed an exquisite rotunda, with stenciled motifs painted on the inside, and historical California murals on the walls.

"Wow. Gorgeous," Hannah said. "Where to?"

At the desk, they checked in with a helpful librarian, and half an hour later, the two were seated at readers, reviewing the papers. Andrea started with the Newport Beach section of the Orange County Register. She scanned the headlines on each page systematically, to be sure she missed nothing. The tiny font was a challenge. There were no rapes reported over Labor Day weekend, but on the following Tuesday, she came across a headline that said

Orange Coast College Co-ed Missing.

Kerry O'Brien, a 19 year old student at Orange Coast Community College, was reported missing by her roommate when she failed to appear for classes on Tuesday morning or for her job as a waitress at a Costa Mesa brewery and restaurant. She was last seen leaving the restaurant after her shift on Saturday night. Anyone with information is asked to contact the Newport Beach police department.

The article was accompanied by a photo of a pert, smiling, blonde.

"Check this out," Andrea said.

Hannah got up and leaned over her shoulder. "Let me look up Tuesday's edition of the other two papers."

The article was repeated in both places. Andrea and Hannah kept scanning for any follow-up. There was no indication that Kerry had ever been found.

Finally, Hannah leaned back in her chair and turned off her terminal. "I think we're wasting our time trying to find anything more this way. If there was a dead body, it could have taken months, or even years, for it to be found. I suggest we enlist Daniel."

Hannah was right. Andrea sighed and stopped reading. At least they'd unearthed one clue that might, or might not, be relevant to Blake's story.

"Thank you, Dr. Watson. How about I take you out for that fabulous lunch?"

CHAPTER TWENTY-SEVEN

Frank Sanderson kept Blake updated daily on Roger's laboratory results, and his PSA levels continued to drop. Blake was jubilant. His brother owed him big time, and he planned to collect.

He arranged to meet Roger for dinner Thursday night at the Beverly Hills Hotel. Roger, who always insisted on the best accommodations, had reserved the legendary Bungalow 3, a favorite of Howard Hughes. The bungalow was furnished like a man cave, with leather-upholstered furniture and dark woods. It was also accessorized with an assortment of vintage model airplanes. A dining table was set and there was a bottle of Cabernet and two glasses on the coffee table. Roger's wheelchair was parked in the foyer, but Roger greeted him at the door with a spring in his step and a smile.

"I thought we'd celebrate my remission and your future financial bonanza," he said.

Blake seated himself and watched as Roger opened the bottle and poured.

"Are you allowed to drink alcohol during treatment?" Blake asked.

"Probably not, but a few sips won't kill me. I've ordered the tasting menu for us tonight. Room service should be here in about half an hour." Roger raised his wineglass, sniffed approvingly, and took a sip.

Blake emulated him and gave a sigh of contentment. It was an exceptional wine. Roger was usually a cheapskate, so he must be really happy.

"I called Dad and told him I was in town having treatment, and that it was working," Roger said.

"Really? What did he say?"

"He said he was glad to hear it, and Mother would be pleased she didn't have to worry about me during Christmas week, when they were going to Maui."

Blake laughed. "It figures. It's always all about them."

Roger shrugged and took another sip of Cabernet.

"I have a question to ask you," Blake said. "That story you told me about the rape...was it true?"

"Why would I lie about it?"

"After you told me, I remembered seeing it, but I wondered if you'd left something out."

Roger's face blanched. "What do you mean, you remembered?"

"I didn't go to bed that night. I was in the pool house, spying on the big boys. I'd forgotten all about it, until I started having these nightmares. It turns out my subconscious has been trying to prod my memory. I'd hoped, once I remembered, that the nightmares would stop, but they haven't. That suggests that there's more to the story."

"That's ridiculous," Roger said. He poured himself some more wine and gulped it down.

"Don't mess with me, brother," Blake said. "If it weren't for me, you'd be in a coffin right now. I'm tired of getting no sleep because of these damned nightmares. Tell me what else happened that night."

Roger put down his wine glass and leaned forward. "In confidence?"

"Of course. All I want is a good night's sleep. If I wanted to fuck you over, all I had to do was to withhold my drug."

"All right. I'll tell you. Let's wait until room service serves dinner and leaves. It's a long story."

Two hours later, Blake shook Roger's hand, thanked him for an excellent meal, and walked to the valet station to retrieve his car. Slipping his hand into his pocket, he removed his phone and shut off the recorder. It never hurt to have insurance, and there were few things as satisfying as now having complete power over his brother.

CHAPTER TWENTY-EIGHT

Andrea got up from her desk, stretched and took a deep breath. The patient light was on. Blake was in the waiting room. He'd left her a cryptic voicemail last night, saying that he'd see her at the usual time. She wished she knew for certain if he had lied or told the truth about the rape. Either way, the story was profoundly disturbing.

She ushered him in, sat down in her armchair, and reached for the mug of tea she'd begun drinking during her last patient session. It was no longer hot, but it gave her something to do with her hands as Blake settled himself.

"So," she said. "You've decided to continue therapy."

From the tense feeling in the pit of her stomach, she recognized that her anxiety about Blake far eclipsed her professional curiosity. Why couldn't he have quit?

"For the time being."

"Did you manage to get any sleep last week?"

"Some," Blake said. "Only one dramatic dream. That's an improvement. I thought about your suggestion that there might be more to what I saw, that I still haven't remembered, and concluded you were probably right."

"Have you remembered any more since I saw you?"

"Not yet. When I remembered the rape, it was like watching a movie. All the images were absolutely clear in my mind, and there was no question that what I remembered was real. The rest of the night is still a blur in my memory, but I know there's more to it. I had dinner with Roger this week, and I forced him to tell me the rest of the story. I don't think he was making it up, but I haven't yet been able to remember that part."

"Tell me what he said."

Blake looked at her with a smug smile. "That's for me to know, and you to find out. I'm not saying anything until my own memories return."

"I see. Well then, tell me this week's bad dream."

"You're gonna love it, Doc. I walked into a church. It was full of people wearing black and I realized I was late for a funeral. Missed all the pompous eulogies. Anyway, everyone was lining up to walk past the casket and say goodbye. I wasn't sure whose funeral it was, but I joined the line. When I got to the casket, I stared at the guy. He looked familiar, but at first, I couldn't place him. Then I realized it was me. It was a very confusing experience. I've never seen myself sleeping and my face looked weird with the eyes closed. Then, I wondered how I died, but there wasn't anyone to ask. Someone closed the casket, and then Roger, my father and a few guys from the funeral home lifted it up and took it to the limousine. Flash forward, the coffin was in a grave, and I was shoveling dirt over it. Roger was watching with a big smile. Then, I woke up."

Andrea didn't say anything. She suspected he had more to tell her and she was happy to wait it out.

"I imagine he was smiling because he'd killed me. I'd made him tell me his deepest, darkest secret. If the situation were reversed, I'd consider murder."

"Are you saying, you've thought seriously about murdering your brother?"

"All the time, when I was a kid. Roger was such a bully. Recently, I've had the occasional fantasy about poisoning his favorite Scotch. My brother's a bit of an alcoholic, but right now, I'm loving being in the position of power. Roger is going to owe every month of his life, from now on, to me. He's my favorite lab rat, and the longer he stays alive, the more successful my drug is going to be."

"Well, I look forward to hearing the next chapter of your recovered memory," Andrea said. "My office will be closed between Christmas and New Year's, so I'll see you on the second Friday in January. Enjoy your holiday."

Thank God, she was going to get some time off from him. She didn't think he was seriously considering murdering his brother. If she had, she would be duty-bound to report it. But at this moment, murder was definitely against Blake's self-interest.

"You too, Doc." Blake did not look happy as he handed her a check and walked out of the office.

When Blake returned to work, there was a call from Dr. Sanderson.

"I wanted to let you know that your brother's PSA has started to plateau. I've sent him for a repeat PET scan, and I'm planning another drug dose next week."

"That sounds like bad news," Blake said.

"Not really. He's had a robust response to the initial therapy. It's not uncommon for the immune system to need another boost. Remember, we don't know the optimum dose for this therapy, and I was being cautious. You need to set up a dose/response trial."

"That's my plan, if Roger's therapy is successful and I can get funding. Keep me posted, will you?"

"I'll forward the lab results and give you a call next week, once I see how Roger is responding."

"You mean you aren't closed for the holiday?" Blake asked.

"Cancer is a twenty-four/seven job. We're on holiday staffing levels but we never close. Maintaining the treatment schedule is too important for patient care."

Obviously, therapy wasn't vital for patient care, or that bitch Andrea would have kept her office open. What made her think taking a holiday should take precedence over Blake's sessions? He ended the call and slammed down the receiver.

Blake didn't understand why his problem was not yet solved and why he couldn't remember the events that Roger had relayed to him. Was it possible that Roger had lied, and Blake didn't remember because Roger's version hadn't happened? When Roger told him about the rape, Blake's memories had been vivid, like watching a movie in Technicolor. He had no doubt that Act One had been real. He was going to have to confront his brother again, so he could remember Act Two and stop dreaming.

It was also time to stop fantasizing about his therapist and to take action. He was planning a romantic getaway for the two of them, and Christmas break was the perfect time. He took a ring of keys from his desk drawer and walked over to the lab. Opening the locked medicine cabinet, he perused his choices, helped himself to a vial of liquid, a large syringe and a needle. Andrea was about to become his lover, whether she wanted to or not.

CHAPTER TWENTY-NINE

Andrea sighed with relief as she entered her house and joined Molly in the den. Molly was on the sofa watching TV, with the kitten on her lap, shedding fur on her jeans, and kneading Molly's new sweater with little claws.

"Hi, Mommy. You look tired. Come watch cartoons with me."

"Sounds like a great idea." Andrea sat down and Molly snuggled into her.

The kitten relocated to Andrea's lap and the sound of purring began; Andrea scratched its ears with one hand, and hugged her daughter with the other.

"I've got a whole week off," she said. "We can think of some fun things to do over dinner."

"Disneyland?"

"Maybe not over Christmas vacation. It'll be packed. We can go there on Superbowl Sunday instead. Everyone will be home watching football and the lines won't be so long."

"Is Daddy off too?" Molly asked.

"We both are, and we need the break. We've been working pretty hard."

Molly snuggled closer. "I love holidays."

~

The landline rang after dinner. Jonathan answered and handed it to Andrea.

"It's Daniel. For you."

"Hi, Daniel. Happy holidays."

"Thanks. I've got a Christmas gift for you, courtesy of the Newport Beach police department. Can I drop it off in twenty minutes?"

"Absolutely."

~

Daniel arrived holding a black loose-leaf notebook, and Andrea drew him into her study.

"Thank you for indulging me," Andrea said.

Daniel handed her the notebook. "I have your answer. The missing woman you read about was found three weeks later, washed up on Laguna Beach. The autopsy showed that she had drowned, but not in the ocean. The water in her lungs was fresh and chlorinated, consistent with a pool. Her body had obviously been dumped."

"Had she been raped?"

"The combination of salt water immersion and being fed on by fishes made that impossible to determine. Can you tell me what you know?"

"I wish I could, Daniel. I can't break patient confidentiality, but I can tell you that what I know and suspect wouldn't hold up in court. You aren't missing out on the opportunity to solve a very cold case."

"I won't press you. Hannah has educated me quite well

on medical confidentiality issues. This is a copy of the murder book, not the original, so you can keep it. Maybe it will help you with your patient."

Andrea gave him a hug and sent her love to Hannah and Zoe.

CHAPTER THIRTY

B LAKE TOSSED AND TURNED ON HIS BED, rearranging the pillows, and trying to quiet his mind. He reached over to his bedside table, and finished off the glass of Scotch he'd been sipping while watching TV. He hated taking pills, but had found alcohol helpful. Finally, he dozed off.

Blake was thirsty again, but he didn't want to miss anything by leaving the window and going to the refrigerator. He kept the slats of the blinds parted, so he could see without being seen. He'd never been so excited.

Roger and his friends had stripped the girl and held her immobile. One of them, at her head, had both wrists in one large hand, while the other covered her mouth so she couldn't scream. One guy held her right leg, another held her left. Blake was in a perfect position to see the bush of blonde hair between them. Roger, the perfect host, had waited until last to take his turn. Blake watched his brother's bare buttocks as he pumped into her.

When he finished, the boys let go and gave one another a high five.

The girl took advantage of the moment, slid off the chaise lounge, and started to run. The guys separated to block her access to the gate at the side of the house. As she ran past the edge of the pool, she tripped on a pair of flip flops and fell into the deep end. A moment later, her head emerged.

Four naked men jumped in and surrounded her. They took turns, pushing her head under water. Each time she emerged, sputtering and cursing. Roger pushed again, holding onto her longer than any of his mates had. Finally, he let go and she came up, lying on her stomach, head in the water.

Roger flipped her over. "Guys, she's not breathing!"

"Shit, let's get her out of here."

The four of them dragged her to the pool stairs, carried her up and laid her on the ground, face up. Roger began breathing into her mouth. Another guy felt for a pulse, and a third pounded on her chest.

Blake watched, a sense of panic in his chest. Was she dead? Had their game killed her?

After a few minutes, Roger lifted his head and shook it. "She's gone."

"Fuck. What do we do now?" One of his companions began to cry.

"We've got to get her out of here. If we dump her body, there won't be any way they can connect her to us," Roger said.

"Except for all the sperm samples we left in her twat," another guy said.

"We can bring her to my dad's boat in the harbor, take it out, and dump the body in the ocean. That should take care of the problem. No one will ever find her," Roger said.

"Good idea. We can wrap her in plastic and put her in the back of my SUV."

"I'll get some." Roger went into the house and returned,

dressed in jeans and a sweatshirt, carrying two large black garbage bags and some rope. Two of his friends pulled the bags over the body and tied them. The guys finished dressing and all four of them carried the body into the garage.

Blake heard the car start and pull into the street. Then there was silence. He emerged from the pool house, shaking with fear. Apart from the disarranged furniture, there was no sign that anything had happened. Maybe this wasn't real. Maybe he'd been having a dream, and he'd wake up and find it was just an ordinary morning, and no one had died. He began to cry with uncontrollable hiccoughs, shaking and wailing.

He woke in his king-sized bed, his face wet with tears. He'd remembered, and it wasn't the version told to him by his son-of-a-bitch brother Roger. This was it, the solution to his months of insomnia. He couldn't wait to confront his brother, and to tell Andrea he no longer needed her as a therapist. If he wasn't her patient, she'd have no excuse. She could leave her husband for Blake, with a clean professional conscience.

CHAPTER THIRTY-ONE

THE MARCUS FAMILY HAD A RELAXING Saturday. Andrea made a picnic lunch, which they ate on a blanket in Crestwood Park, and they took three-year-old Molly to a Disney animated movie. Dinner was pizza at home, on paper plates. Andrea arranged a few play dates for Molly with nursery school classmates, and she and Jonathan planned a leisurely Sunday.

"I'll drop off Molly on my way to the gym, and when I get back, we can drive up to Malibu for a romantic lunch on the beach, and a post-prandial walk along the shore. I made reservations for one o'clock." Andrea said.

"Of course, you did," Jonathan grinned. "How about a post-prandial late afternoon in bed? I can't think of a better stress reducer."

"You're on."

Andrea had never enjoyed traveling during Christmas week. Airports were packed, resorts were crowded, and Christmas carols gave her a headache. She much preferred quiet days at home with her family. She always gave Carla, their housekeeper and nanny, the week off, so that they could have private time. She and Jonathan both needed the break. His work was always stressful, and she couldn't remember a time when her psychiatric practice had felt so tense.

On Sunday morning, she dressed in black yoga pants, a long-sleeved, light-weight top, and a jacket with a zipped pocket for her phone and keys. As she exited the garage with Molly in tow, she looked up and down the street for cars that didn't belong in her residential neighborhood. The streets around UCLA required a resident parking permit and were normally empty. Satisfied that all was well, and shrugging off the sense of unease that she'd had for weeks, she drove the six blocks to Molly's classmate's house, dropped her off, and headed to Equinox.

As she entered the parking lot, she drove up and down the aisles, looking not only for a place to park, but for the Maserati belonging to her patient, Blake Harris. She had identified it the day he'd run into her at the gym, and was pretty sure she could recognize it again. She wanted to avoid another encounter, and how many red Maseratis could there be?

The parking lot was packed, and the only spots were at the far end of the third level. Andrea locked her car and headed inside. She'd start with the elliptical this morning. She really needed some exercise.

CHAPTER THIRTY-TWO

BLAKE HARRIS WATCHED ANDREA DRIVE OUT OF her garage from the comfort of his kitchen. It had been boring and time consuming, when he'd observed her previously from his parked Range Rover. He'd solved that problem a few days ago by installing a tiny, battery-powered camera in an inconspicuous place inside her fence, just opposite the garage door. Reviewing the video on his computer, he could tell by her clothing that she was on her way to the gym. She would probably exercise for about an hour, and it looked as if she was taking the kid somewhere first. Blake had time for a leisurely breakfast and the Sunday television news. He'd arrange things so that he got to the parking lot about half an hour before he expected her to head home. The only tricky part would be finding a spot to park, close to her car. He'd already prepared his syringe of Ketamine, as well as the handcuffs that would keep Andrea immobile while he drove.

Forty-five minutes later, Blake was on his way, driving a black, rented minivan with tinted windows. He'd placed an exercise mat, pillow and blanket in the back. It would take about an hour to get where he was going, and he wanted her to be comfortable, should she wake from the anesthetic early.

Blake was wearing black jeans and a hoodie, wraparound sun glasses, and a beard he'd purchased at a costume store. Even if he was caught on the security cameras, he doubted that he could be identified by facial recognition programs. By 10:45 a.m., most of the gym rats had left and there were plenty of spots. He had no difficulty finding Andrea's Porsche, and was delighted to note that there were empty spots on both sides of her. He backed his van in on her driver's side, making sure he was close enough to her car, so she couldn't open the door all the way. He also left himself plenty of room at the back.

He got out, opened the back doors to his minivan, locked the side doors, made sure he couldn't be seen by anyone entering the lot, and waited with the syringe in his hand.

BOOK 2

DECEMBER 2014

CHAPTER THIRTY-THREE

J ONATHAN, AND THE NEW KITTEN, WERE ensconced in the den on his favorite reclining lounge chair, reading the New York Times. To be accurate, Jonathan was reading and the kitten was practicing shredding. As Jonathan bent over to rescue the Book Review section, he glanced at his watch. It was twelve-thirty. That was odd. Hadn't Andrea said she'd made reservations for one o'clock for lunch? Had he been so absorbed in the paper, he'd failed to hear her come in?

"Andrea? Are you here?"

There was no answer. He climbed the stairs to the master bedroom, but saw no sign that she'd returned. Heading downstairs again, he checked the garage for her car, only to find it wasn't there. She should have been home an hour ago. Reaching for his cell phone, he called and reached voicemail.

"Honey, it's me. Where are you? I'm getting worried."

His next call was to the mother of Molly's play date. "Hi, it's Jonathan. When Andrea dropped Molly off, did she mention any errand she was doing after the gym? She's an hour late getting home and that's not like her."

"She was dressed for a workout. She mentioned the two of you were going to Malibu, and she'd pick Molly up in the late afternoon. She didn't say anything else."

Now, Jonathan was really worried. He grabbed his car keys and drove to the gym. Driving along every aisle of the parking lot, he looked for Andrea's car. He finally found it at the very back of the third story. The gym must have been quite crowded when she'd arrived, but at mid-day, the lot had thinned.

He opened her Porsche with his spare key and noticed a gym bag and jacket in the front seat. Andrea's phone was in the jacket pocket with his voicemail. Where the hell was she?

At the Equinox front desk, he examined the sign-in sheet and noticed that she had arrived at 9:45 a.m. He reached for his phone, found a photo of Andrea, and approached the receptionist.

"Excuse me. I'm trying to reach my wife. She signed in here about three hours ago, hasn't come home, and her car is still in the parking lot with her gym bag in it. I'm worried something might have happened at the gym. Have you seen her?

The receptionist looked at the photo and smiled. "That's Andrea," he said. "I checked her in and saw her leave a little after eleven."

"Was anyone with her?"

"Not that I saw."

Jonathan's mind was racing. Andrea had left the gym and clearly reached her car, because she'd put her gym bag in it. She'd also thrown her jacket with her phone on the passenger seat. She wouldn't have left her phone in the car and risked having it stolen. Something must have happened to her just after she reached the car. He needed access to the gym security tapes. The quickest way to get them was to call Detective Daniel Ross.

CHAPTER THIRTY-FOUR

HANNAH WAS AT THE KITCHEN TABLE, WORKING her way through the Sunday LA Times, when the landline rang. She recognized the number as Jonathan's cell.

"Jonathan, happy holidays."

"Not so happy, Hannah. Andrea is missing. I need to talk to Daniel. Is he home?"

"Hang on. He's in the den." Receiver in hand, she ran to the back of the house and motioned to Daniel to pick up the extension. "It's Jonathan. Andrea's missing."

"Jonathan, what happened?" Daniel said.

Jonathan gave him a recap. "I need you to access the security tapes from the Equinox garage."

"I'll be right there," Daniel said.

"Correction. We'll be right there," Hannah said, hanging up. "Andrea's my closest friend. There is no way I'm sitting home while you investigate."

Daniel didn't argue, just held the door to the garage open for Hannah.

"Don't worry," he said. "We'll find her. I promise."

Hannah nodded. She was confident that she and Daniel

would leave no stone unturned to find Andrea. She just hoped Andrea would be unharmed when they did.

Jonathan had already talked to the security guards at the gym, and was waiting for Daniel and Hannah in the room where the cameras were monitored.

Daniel presented his LAPD Detective's ID and the guard brought up the camera feeds.

"Exactly what time span are you looking for?" he asked.

"My wife signed in at the desk at nine-forty-five, so let's look at the garage entrance starting at nine-thirty, and see when she arrived. She's driving a black Porsche Panamera," Jonathan said.

With three of them looking over the guard's shoulder, they found the car quickly.

"Can we follow her? She parked in the last row of the third level."

The guard switched cameras, and they saw Andrea park and exit her car, dressed in her gym clothes and carrying her gym bag.

"Fast forward, and let's see who else parks in that row."

At 10:45 a.m., a black minivan van with tinted windows backed into the space next to the Porsche. A man emerged, wearing a hoodie, keeping his back to the cameras. Jonathan saw a glimpse of a beard. The man walked to the back of his car and was lost to sight. At 11:10 a.m., Andrea, wearing jeans and a white T-shirt, approached her car and threw her gym bag and jacket into the passenger seat. Then, she rounded the car, looking annoyed, and reached for the handle of the driver's side door, which had been blocked by the bulk of the adjacent minivan.

As Andrea opened the door, the man emerged from

behind his car, disabled her, and shot her with something in a syringe. Andrea appeared to struggle as he pulled her arms back, hoisted her over his shoulder, and forced her into the back of his van. Jonathan caught a glimpse of a bearded face and wrap-around sun glasses. Then, the man climbed into his car and pulled out.

"Oh, my God!" Jonathan said. "She's been kidnapped."

"I can't read the license plate," Daniel said. "It looks like it was smeared with mud. Can we follow the car out and see if we can glimpse the back license, or get a better view of his face?"

The guard switched to other cameras as the car wound down the ramp to the exit.

"Damn," Daniel said. "He's covered up the back license plate as well, and the window is too tinted for a good view of his face."

"He's obviously a planner. This wasn't a spontaneous kidnapping," Hannah said.

"I agree," said Daniel. "I'll need all of those videos. Perhaps our tech guys can extract a license, or a better view of the face, from the recording."

"I'll make a copy of everything and give you the originals," the guard said.

"After we get the files, the three of us need to talk and see if we can figure out who would want to kidnap Andrea," Hannah said.

CHAPTER THIRTY-FIVE

ANDREA AWOKE FEELING NAUSEATED AND WITH a pounding headache. She was in her childhood bedroom in San Francisco, lying on her twin bed with its kitty quilt. She could glimpse the Bay Bridge from the window and a breeze ruffled the sheer white curtains. Across from her bed was her white dresser with its gold knobs and round mirror.

Her father entered the room, smiling at her, and placed a cup of steaming hot chocolate on the bedside table. She could smell it but her stomach rebelled. Her whole body felt peculiar. She reached out her hand to touch him, but he disappeared. She recoiled in horror. Her arm was twice its normal length and her hand was tiny. It was then that she realized that she was missing her left arm.

Shrieking, she jumped out of bed and ran to the mirror. Her face was a distorted horror, as if she'd had bad plastic surgery and couldn't move a muscle. Her hair had been chopped into a buzz cut. Bile rose in her throat, and she looked desperately for a bathroom. She spotted a likely door, and she made it in time to puke into the toilet. Then darkness descended again.

When Andrea regained consciousness, she found herself lying underneath a satin quilt in an unfamiliar bed. The room was dim, with drawn curtains. The only electric light came through a door that was half-open to an adjacent space. Andrea allowed her eyes to adjust and looked around her. She was in a large bedroom with high beamed ceilings, and a fireplace with an ornate French-styled mantel. A flat-screen TV was mounted opposite the bed. Two comfortable armchairs with matching ottomans, upholstered in rose velvet, were arranged in front of the fireplace.

Slowly, she regained control of her limbs and rolled over, turning on a crystal bedside lamp. She pushed away the quilt and sat on the edge of the mattress, waiting for the initial sensation of dizziness to subside. Her head ached and her mouth was dry. She was still wearing her jeans and white T shirt. Her feet were bare, and her sneakers were neatly aligned at the side of the bed. She bent and put them on, finally able to stand.

The room with the light was a bathroom with a huge tub, a glass-walled shower, and his-and-her sinks. She emptied her full bladder and examined herself in the mirror. She looked wasted. Grabbing a washcloth, she washed her face, ran her fingers through her hair and, finding a glass, filled it and quenched her thirst.

Where the hell was she? The last thing she remembered was being grabbed from behind by someone strong, and feeling a needle. Obviously, she'd been abducted and sedated. Looking at her watch, she realized it was after 4:00 p.m. She'd been unconscious for almost five hours. She took a deep breath. She had to stay calm and extricate herself from whatever this was.

Reexamining the bedroom, she looked for her phone, finally remembering it had been in her jacket, which she'd thrown in the car. There was no sign of the jacket anywhere. She opened the mirrored closet doors, just in case, and found herself staring at an almost empty closet with fluffy white terry bathrobes in several sizes. It was reminiscent of a fancy hotel room.

She pushed aside the curtains and looked out. She was on the second floor, with a sheer drop to a stone path that bordered a huge lawn. She could see a circular driveway leading to the house's front door and a set of iron gates in the distance. No exit that way.

Finally, she tested the double doors, gingerly moving the handles to see if they would open. They were locked. It was then that she sunk to the floor, overwhelmed by tears and terror.

CHAPTER THIRTY-SIX

D ANIEL DROPPED OFF THE FILES AT THE WEST LA police station and ushered his two companions into one of the conference rooms.

"Let's pool our information and decide on next steps. This investigation has to be conducted by the book. Any evidence the two of you come across must be collected legally, so it can be used in court when we catch the guy responsible. I'm going to talk to the chief about putting myself in charge, and getting all the help we need, and I'm going to record the information you give me for future reference."

Daniel switched on the recorder and noted the date and time.

"This is Detective Daniel Ross, interviewing Dr. Jonathan Marcus, whose wife, Dr. Andrea Marcus, has just been abducted. Dr. Marcus, can you think of anyone who might have wanted to kidnap your wife?"

"Actually, I can. She recently started seeing a disturbed new patient who frightens her. He's been stalking her, coming on to her sexually, and seems to be in possession of

"

information about her that required him to have investigated her."

"Can you elaborate on that, please? Why did your wife feel she was being stalked?"

"She saw him at Whole Foods, and he also showed up at Equinox, following her from room to room as she exercised. She saw him in the mirror. He then pretended to run into her by accident at the café. He also sent her anonymous flowers on her birthday, a date he shouldn't have known."

"How did she know it was him?"

"She matched the handwriting on the gift card to that on his check."

"Do you have any idea who this man is? The fact that she was kidnapped at Equinox is very suggestive."

"Oh, yes," Jonathan said. "I've met him. His name is Blake Harris. He's the CEO of Chess Pharmaceuticals, a start-up developing immune therapy drugs for cancer. He showed up in our office to persuade one of my partners, Dr. Frank Sanderson, to administer an experimental drug to his brother, who had exhausted all other options. We call it compassionate use and the FDA gives permission."

"So, you've seen him. Did you recognize him on the tape?"

"Not really. All I could see was a hoodie, sunglasses and a beard."

"Any more information you think might be useful?" Daniel asked.

"No, sorry, that's it."

Daniel shut off the recorder. "Hannah, do you have anything to add that might be useful?"

"I think so."

Daniel resumed a formal recording. "This is an interview with Dr. Hannah Kline, the victim's closest friend. What can you tell us?"

"Andrea asked me to help her with some research. Although she was careful to maintain confidentiality, she said she had a patient who claimed to have recovered a memory of witnessing a gang rape when he was a child, over the 1981 Labor Day weekend in Newport Beach. Andrea wondered if there might be anything in the local newspapers to corroborate the reality of the memory."

"What did you find?"

"We found a missing college co-ed whose body was discovered, washed up in Laguna Beach, a few weeks later. You were kind enough to inquire about the missing person case with Newport Beach police, and they sent you a copy of the records. According to the autopsy, this woman died from drowning, but the water in her lungs was consistent with a chlorinated pool. I wasn't told any details about the rape the patient remembered, so I can't say if there is any connection between these two events."

"Did Andrea tell you anything else about her patient?"

"No. She's always discreet."

Daniel ended the interview and took out his notebook.

"Okay, we need to make a to-do list of who to interview and what to search."

"I suggest you talk to Charles Davis. He shares an office with Andrea and functions as her supervisor. I would bet she's told him details about this case. And since she's in danger, and he's our primary suspect, Charles can break confidentiality," Jonathan said.

"How about the guy's brother? He may have some insight into where he might have gone," Hannah suggested.

"Good," Daniel said. "I need to get some search warrants. I want to search Harris's office and home, and find out what other properties he owns. We also need to search Andrea's home and professional office. Ordinarily, I wouldn't need a warrant to search a victim's office, but the rules are different for psychiatrists. The warrant will limit us to records about this specific patient."

"Can't I give you permission to search our home?" Jonathan asked.

"You can, but you can't be involved in the search," Daniel said.

"What about the car?" Jonathan said.

"I've got our tech people working on the video. I'll assign someone to call all the local car rentals to find out if anyone rented this make and model recently."

"So, what's our first step?" Hannah asked.

"I need to see if Mr. Harris is at his office or at home. I think it's unlikely, but it will take some time to get those search warrants. I'm going to talk to the chief now, and ask my partner, Brenda, to get working on the legal stuff and the property search."

"Can we come with you?" Jonathan asked.

"I think it would be best if you waited at home. The husband is usually the prime suspect in cases like this, so you can't be involved in an investigation of your missing wife. A defense attorney would have a field day with that. Anyway, Molly is going to need you with her mother missing."

"I understand." Jonathan looked beaten and forlorn. It obviously hadn't occurred to him that he could be a suspect, hiring someone to get rid of his wife.

Daniel didn't think for one moment that his friend was guilty, but he wasn't going to allow him to mess up his investigation.

"What about me?" Hannah asked.

"Could I keep you away?" Daniel said. He knew better and the last thing he wanted right now was Hannah investigating on her own. "Give me a few minutes to brief my team and let's get going."

CHAPTER THIRTY-SEVEN

URLED UP IN A BALL, ON THE FLOOR NEXT TO the bedroom door, Andrea heard approaching footsteps. She sprung up, wiped her eyes, and sat in one of the armchairs. The last thing she wanted was for her captor to find her terrified and vulnerable. She had to keep her wits about her.

The door opened and Blake appeared in the room, carrying a tray, which he placed on a side table. It contained a flowered teapot, a delicate cup and saucer, a variety of individually-sealed tea bags, and a plate of shortbread cookies.

"You're awake," he said, smiling. "I thought you might like some afternoon tea."

"Blake, where am I and what's going on?"

She wasn't surprised to see him. It made perfect sense that one day he would be unable to resist acting out his fantasies about her. But she couldn't let him see how angry and frightened she was.

"I apologize for ambushing you. I wanted to give you a wonderful vacation, and I was afraid that you'd refuse if I asked you. You would have said you couldn't come with me because of doctor patient rules."

"What was in that shot?"

"Just a little Ketamine, not enough to be dangerous."

That explained the hallucinations.

"It did give me a headache," she said. She worked hard to hide her fury at what he'd done to her.

Blake poured some hot water into the cup and offered her the tea selection. She chose an herbal peach tea and let it steep in the cup.

"Try some shortbread," he urged.

She shook her head. "I'm still nauseated. Just tea will be fine."

She loved shortbread cookies, but she couldn't trust that he hadn't drugged them. For that matter, she'd better not drink too much of the tea. She'd opened the teabag herself, and the water looked clear, but better careful than unconscious again. She'd have to make a point of not eating anything she hadn't seen him eat first.

Andrea removed the tea bag and took a tiny sip. "You still haven't told me where we are."

"We're at my beach house. I'm offering you a week of sand, sun and complete relaxation in my company. By the end of the week, I hope to convince you that life with me is so much more exciting and interesting than the life you live now. You are the smartest and most beautiful woman I've ever known, and I want you with me permanently."

"But Blake, you're my patient," Andrea said.

Why hadn't she anticipated something like this? She knew he was sexually attracted to her, obsessed with her, and he was a man who thought he could have anything he wanted. She should have been more careful.

"Not any more, Doc. You cured me. I've finally remembered all of what happened that night. And I know it's accurate, because I've been sleeping like a baby, ever since. I don't need you as my psychiatrist any longer. You're fired. I much prefer the thought of you as my lover."

This was worse than anything she'd imagined. He'd deluded himself into thinking his attraction to her was mutual, and he obviously had no intention of letting her go. If she said or did anything to anger him, she had no doubt he was capable of rape, and if enraged, of killing her. Psychopaths were unpredictable.

Despite her rage, she had to keep him at arm's length without offending him, to give Jonathan time. She was certain that her husband had already notified Daniel and the LAPD, and that her friends were working full-time to trace her.

"Would you like to tell me what you remembered? If you're crediting me with curing you, I'd love to know how."

Blake settled himself on the chair opposite her and reached for a cookie.

"I'd love to tell you," he said.

CHAPTER THIRTY-EIGHT

"Where to, first?" Hannah asked, as Daniel returned.

It was nice of him not to make a fuss about her coming along. Things had been tense and sad when they'd first returned from their honeymoon, but after their talk, she'd felt calmer and less angry. And now, she sensed that they were truly a team again, on the same page. They had to find Andrea.

"Brenda is working on the search warrants. I called Charles Davis, and he's waiting for us at his home. I thought we'd interview him first."

"Andrea is very fond of Charles. I've never met him, but she thinks he's exceptionally insightful. Let's hope he can fill in some of the blanks for us. Thanks for taking me along."

Daniel smiled. "I think you can really help this investigation. But we've got to work quickly. I'd never forgive myself if..."

"Don't finish that sentence. I can't stand to even think about it," Hannah said.

Daniel pulled the car out of the parking lot and reached over to squeeze her hand. "Me too."

Cheviot Hills was an old neighborhood south of Pico, full of large, charming, old houses, shady trees, and curving streets. Charles and his wife lived in an English Country House, with a formal garden, a bubbling fountain, and cobblestone paths. There was a front porch, with two white Adirondack chairs and several pots of red geraniums.

The door was answered by a slim older woman with chic white hair, wearing light blue slacks, a matching sweater, and silver jewelry. In the background, Daniel could hear the sound of children laughing.

Daniel had called ahead to make sure Charles was home. He'd said he needed some psychiatric input on a case. No point in causing worry prematurely.

The woman smiled. "You must be detective Ross. I'm Carol, Charles's wife. Sorry about the chaos. All the children and grandchildren are here for the afternoon."

"We'll try not to take up too much of Dr. Davis's time," Daniel said. "This is Dr. Hannah Kline, my wife."

Carol held out a hand to Hannah. "Charles is in his study. Let me take you there."

Carol opened Charles's study door and ushered them in. Introductions were made.

"I'll get back to the grandkids," Carol said, closing the door behind her.

"Detective, how can I help you? Is something wrong?" Charles asked.

Daniel sighed. "There isn't any easy way to break this news. Andrea was abducted this morning from the parking lot of her gym. We're mobilizing to find her as quickly as possible, and we thought you might have information that could help us."

"Oh, my God." Charles sat down and hid his face in his hands. He was devastated. He loved Andrea like a daughter, and couldn't bear the thought that she could be hurt, or worse.

"Please, tell me what you know, and how this happened," he begged Daniel.

Daniel took a disc out of his breast pocket. "I'll show you the security tapes. Tell me if you recognize this man."

Charles put the disc in his computer and Daniel fast forwarded it to the relevant portion.

"Have you ever seen him before?"

"I can't say I have. He looks as if he's gone to great lengths not to be recognized."

"Not in your office waiting room?" Hannah asked.

Charles shook his head. "Andrea and I stagger our patients, so that they don't meet one another. I rarely see any of hers."

"Jonathan suspects a patient who has been stalking her. Do you know anything about that?" Daniel asked.

"Yes, I do, and I think Jonathan may be right. From everything Andrea told me, the patient fits the criteria of a psychopath."

Charles did not hesitate to elaborate on everything she told him, the dreams, the stalking, the hostility, the efforts to control her, Andrea's initial dislike evolving into fear, the rape dream and recovered memory, and Andrea's conviction that there might be more to the story, not yet in conscious memory. Confidentiality was irrelevant if Andrea's life was in danger.

"The only thing I don't know is his name," Charles said. "But we should be able to find that in Andrea's office records."

"We know his name," Daniel said. "We're waiting for an official warrant to search her office."

"I hope it comes through soon," Charles said. "I have a spare key I can give you, so you won't have to find the security guard or break in."

He opened a desk drawer, handed Daniel a keychain with three keys, and walked Daniel and Hannah to the door. "Let me know immediately if you find her, or if you think of anything else I can do to help. Anything at all."

CHAPTER THIRTY-NINE

DANIEL AND HANNAH RETURNED TO DANIEL'S car just as his cell rang.

"It's Brenda," he said, answering it.

He listened for a moment and said "Great, I'll meet you in front of Harris's apartment building in fifteen minutes."

He hung up, started the car, and reversed out of the driveway. "We've got all the warrants. Brenda is bringing them to me, along with a backup team. I doubt he's in his apartment with Andrea. That would be too easy. But if he is, he could be armed. I can't let you participate in searching his home, but I was hoping you'd accompany Brenda to Andrea's house and office. You know her so well, you might easily spot something Brenda would miss."

He was hoping she'd go along with his plan and not berate him for being overprotective. By now, she should know the rules. There was no way he could let a civilian (especially his wife) be involved in searching this suspect's home.

"No problem. If Brenda has no objection, I'll go with her

and see if I can find the relevant files. Don't worry, I won't read them."

"It never occurred to me that you would. When you're done, have Brenda call me. She can drop you off at home on her way back to the station. Can you go pick up Zoe from her playdate?"

"Of course. I'll see you later."

Daniel pulled up in front of the Wilshire Boulevard high-rise where Harris lived. Brenda was waiting for him, driving a black and white. There were two more black-and-whites parked behind her, each with two patrolmen. She got out of her car and handed Daniel a manila envelope.

He pulled the warrants for Andrea's home and office, and gave them to Brenda. "Can you start here? You're looking for any material related to Blake Harris. I asked Hannah to go with you. She knows how Andrea thinks and should be helpful."

Brenda smiled. "Come on, Hannah. I'd have preferred lunch and a movie, but this will have to do for a girl's afternoon."

CHAPTER FORTY

NDREA HADN'T FOOLED BLAKE FOR A MINUTE. Underneath the cool demeanor, he could sense her fear. Not to mention the fact that her eyes were red and swollen. He had every intention of keeping her, with or without her consent, but he preferred to woo her and tame her, so that she yielded to his will in all things.

"You want to know what I remembered?" he said. "Let me tell you first what Roger told me."

She leaned forward, looking at him with interest.

"I told Roger I was sure something else had happened that night and demanded he tell me. He said that after the rape, as he and his friends were putting their clothes back on, the girl made a run for the beach. He and another guy chased her, but she ran into the ocean and began swimming. After a few minutes, they lost sight of her. They'd all been very nervous that when she emerged from the ocean, naked, she would report them to the police, but nothing ever happened. A few weeks later, there was an article in the paper about her disappearance. They figured she'd drowned. Roger felt bad, but was also relieved that he hadn't gotten himself and his friends in deep trouble."

"Did you believe his story?" Andrea asked.

"I did at first, but when it didn't jog my memory and the nightmares kept coming, I realized he'd fed me a load of crap. I was about to threaten to cut off his drug supply when I remembered what really happened."

"Are you sure about that memory?"

"Positive. It was like seeing it in Technicolor on a high-def TV, after viewing something in black-and-white on a 1950s twelve inch. It felt absolutely right, and as proof, the nightmares stopped."

"Can you describe the memory?"

"Absolutely. After the rape, the four of them ignored her and started putting their clothes back on. She got up off the deck and began backing away from them. Roger noticed and ran toward her, which resulted in her losing her balance at the edge of the pool and falling in. I saw her head bob up and she started swimming toward the other end. Roger and his friends stopped dressing and ran for the pool. They jumped in and surrounded her. Roger pushed her head under, and each time she fought her way up, someone else pushed her down again, and held her there. After the third or fourth time, she came up floating on her belly, and they must have realized the game had gone too far. They pulled her out of the pool and tried CPR. I didn't know what that was at the time, but I remember someone beating at her chest, and Roger looking as if he was kissing her. When she didn't move, the four of them argued."

"Finally, Roger went into the house and came out with two big, black plastic garbage bags. They placed her inside and carried her into the garage. I heard a car start and exit the gates. After that, I went back to my room. I figured they'd gone to bury her somewhere."

"Did you ever find out what they did with her?" Andrea's face looked drained of blood.

He'd known she would freak out when he told her the story. "I don't know, but either she's in a hole somewhere, or they dumped her in the ocean from my Dad's boat. That might have been easier. Roger's always been a lazy SOB. He probably didn't have the energy to dig a grave."

"That must have been horrible for you to watch at that age. No wonder you suppressed it," Andrea said.

Her face actually looked sympathetic. He should probably play into that.

"It was the worst thing I'd ever seen," Blake said, allowing his voice to crack. "Roger doesn't deserve my drug. If I had remembered this in time, I'd have refused."

"Have you thought about telling the police?"

"The police are too dumb to believe me and it's not worth it now. Even if my drug gives him a temporary lease on life, he'll die soon anyway. Justice will be served." Blake got up. "I should let you rest for awhile. I've arranged for a very special dinner at eight o'clock, and I have a surprise for you."

He walked to the door and opened it, retrieving several Nieman Marcus shopping bags that he'd left in the hallway.

"I know you didn't have a chance to pack for this trip, so I got you a few outfits to wear for the week. Put on something special for tonight."

He smiled at her again and left the room, locking the door behind him.

CHAPTER FORTY-ONE

D ANIEL WALKED INTO THE LOBBY OF BLAKE Harris's building and stopped at the concierge desk.

"I'm here to see Blake Harris," he said.

"I don't believe Mr. Harris is at home," the concierge answered. "I saw him leave this morning with a suitcase and I haven't seen him return."

"What time did he leave?"

"I think it was around ten."

Daniel took out his ID. "I'm Detective Daniel Ross of the LAPD. I have a warrant to search Mr. Harris's apartment. I assume you have a passkey." He handed over the paperwork.

"Yes, sir. I do." The concierge retrieved a ring of keys.

Daniel walked back to the front entrance and motioned for his team to come in. Four armed policemen followed him to the elevator. The nervous concierge entered after the group.

The elevator stopped at the Penthouse level and the concierge opened the door.

"Mr. Harris, are you there? It's Eddie." There was no answer.

"Thanks, Eddie. You can go now," Daniel said.

The four policemen cleared the apartment. "No one's here, Detective."

Daniel hadn't expected to find Andrea in Harris's apartment, but he still felt a twinge of disappointment. "Let's do a quick search, secure the electronics, and I'll send in a forensic team if we find anything suspicious."

The apartment was spacious, with views to the south and west. The great room contained a kitchen and breakfast area, and a large living space with a huge TV and a fireplace. Daniel noticed used breakfast dishes on the table as well as a computer. He sent the others to check out the bedrooms and sat down at the computer. It woke when he moved the mouse, but as expected, it was password protected. He should probably pack it up and bring it to Izzy, their IT specialist at the station, rather than wasting his time trying to guess the password.

On the other hand, he did have one idea. He took out his phone and called Jonathan.

"You wouldn't happen to know the name of the miracle drug Harris developed?" Daniel asked.

"Not offhand, but I can call my partner and get it for you. Is it important?"

"I don't know yet, but I'd appreciate your help."

A few minutes later he got a text: *BLAKIMAB*

Daniel tried a few variations of capital and small letters before succeeding with *BlakImab*. It had been worth his time after all.

The screen opened to a video of the Marcus's garage. He scrolled backwards and saw Andrea, dressed in workout clothes, and Molly, leaving in Andrea's Porsche at a little after nine o'clock.

He called Brenda. "When you get to Andrea's house, look for a small camera facing the garage. Our suspect has been spying on her."

"So, it was him."

"Looks like it."

Daniel opened all the videos in the file folder and found that Harris had been following Andrea's movements for at least a week.

"Hey, Daniel. You need to see this," someone called from the bedroom.

The bedroom was sparsely furnished with a king-sized bed and a wall of mirrors. A dresser drawer was open, filled with handcuffs, collars, whips and other S&M paraphernalia. "Looks like our guy has kinky sexual tastes."

"Any sign of blood anywhere?" Daniel asked.

"No," one of the other cops said from the bathroom. "But look what I found in the trash basket."

There was a torn wrapper from a 10cc syringe and another from an 18-gauge spinal needle. An empty box, labeled Ketamine, lay next to them.

"There's a half-empty vial of the stuff on the sink. I'll put all of this in an evidence bag."

"Okay," Daniel said. "We've found enough to confirm that we are on the right track. I'd like one of you to stay here and wait for the forensic team. The rest of you, come with me. We need to go to his office and see if he's holding Andrea there."

CHAPTER FORTY-TWO

WHEN BLAKE LEFT, ANDREA WENT TO THE bathroom and locked the door. She was desperate for a shower and didn't want to be interrupted. She turned it on to as hot a temperature as she could tolerate, helped herself to shampoo, body scrub and cream rinse, and stood crying under the hard spray. When she was out of tears, she turned the shower off, wrapped herself in a fluffy white bath towel, and borrowed a round brush and hair dryer from a bathroom drawer. The drawer also contained new makeup supplies, clearly unused. There was a silk kimono hanging on a hook in back of the door and she put it on. She wondered who all this stuff belonged to.

Had Blake lied to her about having a wife or girlfriend? Did he keep this bedroom supplied with extras for women he kidnapped? Or had he been planning this for so long, he had outfitted the room specifically for her? The last thought made her nauseous.

Returning to the bedroom, she explored the bags Blake had given her from Neiman Marcus. One bag held delicate La Perla underwear, panties and bras. He'd guessed well.

The sizes were correct. The thought that he'd been mentally measuring her breasts felt creepy. There was also a sheer white silk nightgown—very virginal.

The second bag held an assortment of tights, jeans, T-shirts and socks. Once again, he had assessed her size correctly. She dressed in a pair of black tights and an olive shirt. The third bag had a pair of black suede boots and a warm black sweatshirt.

A fourth bag held swimsuits and flip flops. The fifth bag contained two designer dresses. One was long, black and sleeveless, with a deep cleavage. The second was dark green with a high neck and a low back. Along with the dresses was a pair of Christian Louboutin stiletto heels. She was hoping they wouldn't fit, but when she slipped them on, they were perfect.

The final, smallest bag was from Tiffany. It contained a black velvet box with a diamond necklace and a pair of diamond stud earrings. She estimated each one was at least four carats. Clearly, he thought he could buy her.

Now that she was dressed, and her head was beginning to clear, she decided to do a more careful search of the room. The dressers were empty. The drawer in one of the bedside tables contained a box of condoms and lubrication. She shivered.

Opening the closet, she put away the clothes. She needed to spend the next few hours deciding how she was going to get out of this situation.

CHAPTER FORTY-THREE

D ANIEL AND HIS TEAM DROVE UP TO THE building containing Chess Pharmaceuticals. He told one of the cops to cover the back entrance and approached the front door. It was locked, but a security guard sat at a desk inside watching a monitor. Daniel knocked to get his attention.

"The building's closed for the weekend," the guard said. "Come back Monday."

"Police," Daniel said, flashing his ID. "We have a search warrant for Chess Pharmaceuticals. Anybody up there now?"

The guard opened the door and let them in. "No one's in the whole building. Chess is on the fourth floor."

"You got a passkey?" Daniel asked.

"I can let you in with my card," he said.

Daniel and two cops accompanied the guard to the fourth floor, and waited for him to unlock the door. Then, Daniel told him to go back downstairs. As soon as the elevator door closed, the men drew their guns and cautiously cleared the space.

No one was there. The company consisted of an unassuming waiting room, a large room full of cages with rats in various states of disease, and a large office for the CEO. They searched all the drawers and confiscated the computer. Daniel tried variations on the *BlakImab* passcode and was pleased to find one that worked. He didn't bother exploring the files. He'd drop it off at the station and let the IT guys have a look.

Hannah and Brenda made their first stop at Andrea's home. Brenda handed Jonathan the official search warrant and Hannah gave him a hug. He looked shattered.

"Any news?"

"Not yet, but Daniel's mobilized a large team to help. When do you have to pick up Molly?"

"I've arranged for her to have a sleepover with her friend. She's a smart kid, and I don't want her seeing how worried I am. I'm hoping we'll know something by tomorrow."

"I'm sure we will. Daniel has practically the entire West LA division working on it," Hannah said.

"Hannah," Brenda said, "why don't you go to Andrea's study and see if you can find anything pertinent to our suspect. I'm going outside to the garage."

Jonathan looked puzzled and glanced at Hannah, but neither she nor Brenda enlightened him. He didn't need to know that there was a camera hidden on his property. Poor guy had enough to worry about.

"Why don't you wait for me in the kitchen?" Hannah suggested. "We can have a cold drink when I finish looking through Andrea's files."

"You can't read Andrea's private files!" Jonathan protested.

"I know that. There's only one file I'm looking for and it belongs to the suspect. It's probably in her office, not at home, but I need to check, and I wouldn't read that one either. I'm not a law enforcement agent and I'm well aware of HIPAA rules. Trust me."

"I do. I'm sorry," Jonathan said. His eyes filled with tears."

Andrea's study was bright, cheerful and very personal. Family photos lined the walls. A cork board held drawings by Molly. The shelves were painted white and full of recreational reading. There was a two-drawer file cabinet and a white oak desk, which held Andrea's laptop and her in-and-out tray.

Hannah flipped through file folder labels, finding mostly financial files and binders with psychiatry course information. There was no patient information. However, the murder book Daniel had given her was on the desktop. Hannah retrieved it. Perhaps it might be helpful.

She returned to the kitchen, where Jonathan handed her a glass of sparkling water.

A few minutes later, Brenda came in. "I think we're done here."

Hannah got up and kissed Jonathan on the cheek. "I'll keep you posted. I promise."

Once they reached the car, she turned to Brenda. "Did you find it?"

"Found and disabled it. It's in an evidence bag. Hopefully, it'll have some fingerprints."

"Charles gave me Andrea's office keys," Hannah said.

"Let's go," Brenda replied.

It was a five minute drive to Andrea's office. Hannah opened the door and they entered the well-appointed waiting room.

"Did you find anything of value in her home study?" Brenda asked.

"Just the murder book Daniel gave us. It's in my tote bag. I thought he might find it useful."

"What murder book?"

"I helped Andrea research a possible rape or missing woman in Orange County, over Labor Day weekend, in 1981. We found a reference and asked Daniel to see if the police ever found her. Apparently, she washed up on the beach a few weeks later, and it was clear she had been murdered. They never solved the crime. Andrea suspected the murder might have something to do with information she'd gotten from a patient in therapy, but she didn't tell me the details. The Newport Beach police gave Daniel a copy of the murder book. We still don't know if this murder is connected to Andrea's kidnapping, but given the current situation, I brought it with me."

"Let's hope we find some records in her office that will help," Brenda said.

Hannah found the key to Andrea's consultation room, and the two women entered.

"I want to check the computer and the desk drawers. You take the file cabinet," Brenda said.

"You won't find any patient records on Andrea's computer," Hannah said. "She's paranoid about being hacked and about protecting her patients' privacy."

"Maybe not, but perhaps our suspect sent her emails or photos. I have to bring the computer in, regardless."

"I know." Hannah winced at the thought of Andrea's privacy being violated at the police station, but this was an emergency. Anything that could help find her had to be unearthed.

As she expected, the file cabinet was locked, but it yielded to the third key on the ring Charles had given her. The top drawer contained patient files. Hannah skipped quickly to the folder labeled "H" and found Blake Harris.

"Got it." She handed it to Brenda, who placed it in an evidence bag, after also bagging the murder book.

"What now?"

"I'm dropping you off at home and I'm taking everything to the station. Daniel's called a team meeting to compare notes."

"Do I have to go home?" Hannah asked.

"If it were up to me, I'd be happy to include you, but the captain would never agree to having a civilian in a team meeting. I'm sorry, Hannah. I know she's your closest friend. But I'm sure Daniel will keep you in the loop."

"He'd better," Hannah said, as she locked the door.

CHAPTER FORTY-FOUR

ANDREA OPENED HER EYES, SURPRISED THAT she had drifted off to sleep in the armchair. Her watch said 7:10 p.m. Blake had told her to be dressed for dinner by 8:00 p.m., and she decided to comply. She needed to pick her battles and this wasn't one of them.

She chose the green dress. It was better to avoid the one with cleavage. Then she slipped her bare feet into the stilettos. Blake had provided stockings and a lacy black garter belt, but there was no way she was going to wear them. She brushed out her hair and applied a small amount of subtle makeup: powder, blush, lip gloss and a touch of mascara. He wanted her to look glamorous. No point in looking haggard and making him angry, or aware of how she was really feeling.

Promptly at 8:00 p.m., Blake knocked on the door.

"Come in," she said.

This was pointless of course. He had the key.

Blake opened the door, dressed in a tuxedo. He gave her a wide smile. "You look ravishing. But haven't you forgotten something?"

"I don't think so."

"The outfit would look so much better with jewelry."

"I'm not comfortable wearing anything that expensive," Andrea said. "I'd be afraid of losing it. Can we go to dinner now? I'm hungry."

Blake frowned but let it go. He held out his arm to her and she took it. He led her down a carpeted corridor to a sweeping double stairway, and into a formal dining room.

The furniture was mahogany with a Chinoiserie buffet and upholstered chairs. The walls were covered in peach silk and adorned with a collection of Japanese prints. There were two lavish table settings at one end: English china, baroque sterling and sparkling Waterford wine and water glasses. Several covered dishes sat on the buffet.

Blake pulled out a chair for her and served her a salad plate. The salad consisted of baby greens, fresh strawberries, goat cheese and pistachios. She waited for him to serve himself and take the first bite. The salad was delicious.

"Did you make this?" Andrea asked.

"Not exactly. I had a private chef here, preparing meals for us while you were resting. I wanted everything to be perfect for you."

The only perfect thing Andrea could think of was having a phone so she could call a taxi and escape from this surreal nightmare. She wasn't really hungry. Her stomach was churning with fear and anxiety.

Blake cleared the salad plates and brought her a veal chop, sitting on a bed of whipped butternut squash. "Can I pour you some wine?"

A bottle of expensive Brunello was sitting open and airing on the table. "I'd better not. I don't think alcohol mixes well with Ketamine, and I still feel a little nauseated and have a headache."

"I apologize. It was the only way I could think of to get you here. I promise, from now on, things will be different."

"Different how?"

"I've planned a romantic week for you. Tomorrow, we'll walk on the beach. We can watch movies in our home theater. It's a bit chilly for the pool, but we can go in the hot tub, and of course, we're going to have the most exciting sex you've ever experienced."

The thought of sex with Blake made her even more nauseous. She had to figure out some way to stop him.

"I won't rush you. I'm playing for keeps. And I promise that, by the end of the week, you'll be happy to tell your husband you're with me now."

"My husband is probably frantic with worry right now. I wouldn't be surprised if he's reported me missing to the police."

"That's why, after dinner, you're going to email him and tell him you've run off with another man, and not to bother looking for you."

Did he really think Jonathan would believe that? But it was an opportunity. She could word it so that he'd know she'd written it under duress.

CHAPTER FORTY-FIVE

A FTER DINNER, BLAKE ESCORTED HER INTO A study. He booted up the desk computer and logged into a site on the dark web. Andrea's email would be routed through a dozen different portals and be impossible to trace. He motioned for her to sit down.

"You type. I'll dictate," he said, standing over her shoulder.

Dear Jonathan,

I apologize if you were worried about me, but I am safe and well. I've left you for someone else, and will be back in a week or so to negotiate our divorce.

Andrea paused. "I have to say something about our daughter, or he won't believe the email is really from me."

"Go ahead." Blake watched her every keystroke. There was no way she could send anything he didn't approve.

We'll need to arrange for joint custody for Melissa. My lawyer will be in touch.

Andrea

She hit SEND.

Blake was satisfied. He knew winning her wasn't going to be easy, but this was a good first step. He'd take her back to her bedroom and let her get some sleep. Tomorrow was soon enough to teach her how to be sexually submissive.

Blake escorted Andrea to her room and she heard him lock the door. Of course, he could unlock it at any time while she was sleeping and she would be helpless.

She spotted a chair in front of a small desk in the corner, and wedged it underneath the doorknob. She wasn't certain it would protect her from an unwanted nighttime visit, but it was the best she could do.

She removed her clothing, put on tights and a t-shirt, and lay down under the warm quilt, leaving the bathroom door open as a night light. Getting to sleep wasn't going to be easy, but it was essential if she was going to be able to keep her wits about her the next day. She had no illusions about the tightrope she was walking. One misstep, and she could unleash his rage and find herself beaten, raped or even killed. If only Jonathan and the police could find her before that happened.

CHAPTER FORTY-SIX

I T WAS DARK BY THE TIME THE TEAM assembled and reported in. Daniel turned over the computers to Isidore Washington, Izzy, for short, the LAPD's most skillful technology specialist.

"We have excellent evidence that Blake Harris is responsible for the kidnapping," Daniel announced. "We found an empty syringe and bottle of Ketamine in his apartment, as well as videos that prove he was stalking Andrea Marcus. Unfortunately, Andrea wasn't in the apartment or at his office. What do we know about the black minivan?"

Diego, a young Latino cop, spoke up. "I traced it to an Enterprise rental in Inglewood. Blake Harris rented it for two weeks and paid in cash. He obviously wanted to avoid using a credit card, but couldn't use a fake name because he needed to give them his driver's license and proof of insurance. Maybe he thought we wouldn't find it because it was rented far from his neighborhood."

"Good work. Where are we at tracing his properties?"

"I worked on that," said Alicia, a new hire just out of the Academy. "Blake Harris owns three properties in his name, and there's also a Harris Family Trust which owns several more." She passed around a sheet of paper. "Blake has a condominium in Aspen and a house in Del Mar, in addition to his apartment in Westwood. The family trust has a home in Newport Beach, which is their main residence, an apartment in New York, a place in North Lake Tahoe, a house on Maui, and a villa in the South of France."

"I don't think he would have taken her anywhere that involves flying," Brenda said. "Flights are too easy to trace and he couldn't risk going through a security line with her."

"I agree," Daniel said. "The most likely possibility is Del Mar or some motel, off the beaten track. Let's put out a BOLO for the rental car, now that we have a plate. Brenda, ask San Diego PD to see if the car is at the house or if the house appears occupied. Diego, you ask Tahoe police to do the same."

"They might not be in Tahoe yet," Brenda said. "It's a long drive and there's been a great deal of snow in that area."

Daniel nodded. "You're right. We'll have to check motels along Route 5, as well. If he was planning to take her to Tahoe, he could have stopped for the night."

"What about Newport Beach?" Alicia asked.

"That's less likely. His parents live there," Daniel said.

"Unless they've gone to the South of France for the holidays," Brenda said.

"True. I'll call the Newport Beach police and have them recon the place. Remind each police department you speak to that this is a hostage situation. They could put Andrea in danger if they go off half-cocked. If one of these houses seems occupied, they need to stand down and report back to us. In the meantime, we need to come up with a safe strategy for getting her out."

CHAPTER FORTY-SEVEN

ANDREA WOKE A LITTLE BEFORE DAWN, TOOK A quick shower and dressed. It didn't appear that Blake had tried to break into her room, but she wanted to be sure she was alert and had her clothes on before he appeared. No way was she going to let him find her in bed and vulnerable. When she was sure she was ready, she removed the chair from under the doorknob and seated herself in one of the comfortable armchairs.

She wished she had something to read. It would occupy her mind and keep her from visualizing scenarios of Blake acting out his fantasies on her. As his therapist, she had a good idea of what those fantasies might be and they terrified her.

The morning light grew brighter through the windows of her room, and finally, at a little after eight in the morning, Blake knocked at her door.

"Come in," she said.

Blake was wearing jeans and a long-sleeved black sweater. She would have found the exterior attractive if she didn't know what lurked inside.

"I never figured you for an early riser," he said. "I was concerned I might wake you."

"I do my best thinking in the morning," she said. "Any chance of coffee and the Los Angeles Times?"

"Your wish is my command. Breakfast is served."

He guided her downstairs. This time, he took her through a set of glass doors to the outside patio and pool. A table was set with fresh orange juice, a coffee pot, and a basket of French breakfast pastries.

"If you'd like eggs or cereal, just let me know," he said, as he pulled out a chair for her.

"This is perfect. Thank you." It was going to be a beautiful day, but this early, it was still cool out on the patio. Andrea was glad she'd dressed warmly and had put on the black sweatshirt.

"Our stretch of the beach is almost private, especially in the morning and during off-season," Blake said. "We'll take a walk after breakfast."

"Good. I could use some exercise," she answered. The longer she could keep him outdoors, the better. She was certain he was planning something sexual once they went back inside, and the thought panicked her. The only thing she had going for her was that he was in a courting mode. He would want, at least initially, to please her, and that might help her keep him at arm's length, and buy time for the LAPD to trace her.

CHAPTER FORTY-EIGHT

AFTER A VERY LATE NIGHT, DANIEL ALSO WOKE before dawn.

Hannah rolled over and sat up in bed. "What are you planning today? Any progress on the case?"

He looked at her, hair tousled from sleep, wearing a long-sleeved white nightgown, and he wanted nothing more than to go back to bed, make love to her, and pretend that nothing was wrong. He knew better.

Sitting on the edge of her side of the bed, he brought her up to date.

"We were on the phone checking motels all along I-5. No luck. Neither the Tahoe, San Diego or Newport Beach police saw Harris's car near the homes he could be using, but all the houses have garages. They're staking them out to see if there's any activity during the day."

"What's your next move?"

"Brenda and I are going to interview Roger Harris, the brother, and see what he knows."

Hannah reached out and grabbed his arm. "Keep me in the loop. I'm a wreck."

"I know you are." Just then, his cell phone rang.

It was Jonathan.

"Have you heard anything?" Daniel asked.

"I got an email from her."

"What does it say?"

"It says she's left me for another man, and will be home next week to work out our divorce and custody arrangements for Melissa."

"Melissa?"

"That's how I know she was forced to write it. I'm sure that using the wrong name for Molly was her way of telling me not to believe what I'm reading."

"I think you're right. Can you bring your computer to the station? I'll see if Izzy can trace the email."

Daniel hung up, bent down and kissed Hannah's cheek. "I'll call you later. I promise."

CHAPTER FORTY-NINE

IT WAS A PERFECT MORNING FOR A BEACH WALK. The sky was clear, the waves rolled in a long line, designed for surfing, and the beach was deserted. In the distance, Blake could see people walking their dogs or jogging near the high tide line, but his end of the beach was hard to access unless you knew where the narrow right of way was located. The rich property owners didn't want their tranquility disturbed by people who didn't belong.

Andrea walked briskly by his side, hood up, hands in her pockets, eyes squinting slightly as the sun became brighter. He hadn't thought to purchase sun glasses for her. Perhaps he could find an extra pair in his mother's dressing table.

He liked the fact that she was fit, and kept up with him despite his longer stride. He could see the muscles of her legs contracting under the slim jeans she wore and he imagined those legs locked around his buttocks as he plunged into her. He could feel himself getting hard, just thinking about it.

They'd have to turn around in a few minutes. He didn't want her getting too close to other people.

"Let's stop here for a break," he said, seating himself on a long driftwood log. She joined him, putting distance between them, and catching her breath.

"I see why you like it here. It's very calming," she said.

"I'm glad you appreciate it. When we get back, I'll introduce you to my hot tub. It's the perfect end to a brisk, cool, beach walk."

She didn't reply. She was probably trying to figure out which of the bikinis he'd purchased she should put on. Personally, he liked to go in bare-assed. Maybe for their first time, he'd rip off her bikini bottoms and take her in the tub. Then he'd introduce her to his well-equipped bedroom. He wondered how long it would take her to submit, and when she'd make the connection between eroticism and pain. He suspected she'd be a challenge.

Andrea rose and stretched out her hamstrings. Then she pulled off her socks and sneakers, and ran toward the water, splashing in the ends of the breaking waves. She smiled at him.

"Get your feet wet. It feels great."

Wet feet, and wet pants, did not appeal to Blake, but he followed her. The water was icy. He noticed that her jeans were wet from her knees down. She'd probably insist on drying off before they walked back. He found this annoying. He had a schedule in mind and she'd just delayed him. It wouldn't do her any good. It was just making him hotter for her, and he'd have to devise an additional punishment to teach her not to interfere with his plans.

Blake wished he could find out how Jonathan had reacted to Andrea's email. Had he believed her, and consulted a lawyer, or had he gone to the police?

CHAPTER FIFTY

Daniel presented his ID at the registration desk of the Beverly Hills Hotel and got directions to Roger Harris's bungalow.

His knock was answered by Roger's attendant.

"I'm Daniel Ross, LAPD. I need to see Mr. Harris."

"Mr. Harris is still sleeping."

"Wake him up. Tell him it's important. I'll come in and wait." Daniel held the door open and pushed past the aide. He raised his eyebrows, observing the dark wood and leather room with its elaborate collection of model planes. He remembered crafting planes as a teenager, and would have loved to examine them, but he seated himself on an armchair instead, facing the bedroom.

The aide knocked softly, and hearing no reply, entered the room and closed the door. A few minutes later, he came out.

"Mr. Harris is getting up and putting on some clothes. He'll be with you as soon as he's taken his medications."

The attendant retrieved a wheelchair from the corner of the room and rolled it into the bedroom. Daniel waited.

He was shocked when Roger Harris emerged. Roger's face was skeletal, his hair gone. He was wearing a white T-shirt and a plaid blanket covered his legs. An extensive rash showed on both arms and his face. His complexion was jaundiced and his breathing fast and shallow.

"Order some coffee," Roger said to his attendant. Then he turned to Daniel. "Sorry to keep you waiting. What is this about?"

"It's about your brother, Blake. He's missing. He disappeared early yesterday, his phone is off, and he's not in his office or his apartment. Blake is a witness in a case we're investigating and we need to get in touch with him. Do you have any idea of where he might have gone to ground?"

"It's not like Blake to be separated from his phone. He's a world class workaholic. Do you think he's dead, or in danger?"

"We don't know. I thought you could help us find him."

Roger paused to catch his breath. "He's got two vacation homes within driving distance, or he could have flown to the South of France. The parents own a villa they're not using at the moment. They're in Maui, while I'm here being a lab rat for Blake."

"Could he have gone to their home?"

"I suppose, although he usually avoids the place like the plague. Neither of us is fond of the parents."

"You said you were a lab rat?" Daniel asked.

"Yeah. He's trying his new immune therapy drug on me. It's supposed to cure metastatic prostate cancer. I was doing great until last week, when I developed this rash and got short of breath." He looked at his Rolex. "I'm supposed to be at the cancer center this morning. I have a feeling Blake's pet project is failing."

"When was the last time you saw your brother?"

"I think it was about a week ago. He came here and we had dinner."

"Did he talk about any plan to leave town?" Daniel asked.

"Not really. He was keeping an eye on my therapy. Wanted to make sure his potentially blockbuster drug actually worked."

"Where are you being treated?"

"Doctor Frank Sanderson is the oncologist who is working with me. He's on staff at Memorial Hospital."

"Thank you, Mr. Harris. I don't want to keep you from your doctor's appointment."

"Let me know if you find my brother," Roger said.

As Daniel returned to his car, his cell rang. The Newport Beach police department had assigned two officers to stake out the house. One of them was observing, with a pair of binoculars, while walking his dog. He reported a man and a woman, meeting the description, exiting the house and walking on the beach.

"Great to know. At least she's alive. Don't approach. The guy's a psychopath. We can't risk doing anything that might make him hurt or kill her. I'll bring my team and coordinate with your department. We'll need to brainstorm a strategy for getting him away from her, so we can affect a rescue. Expect us within the hour."

Daniel put on his siren and gunned the gas, making a quick call to Brenda so that the team would be armed and ready to leave when he got there. Then, as promised, he called Hannah.

CHAPTER FIFTY-ONE

TEARS WERE RUNNING DOWN HANNAH'S cheeks. They were tears of temporary relief. She'd been a wreck for hours, waiting for Daniel's call.

"I was so scared she was dead."

"I know," Daniel said. "But the Newport Beach police spotted her on the shore, with her kidnapper. Apparently, he's brought her to his parent's house on Sandstone Drive. I just finished interviewing Harris's brother, Roger. He told me their parents were in Maui."

"Can you get her out of there?"

"I'm heading down there now with a team and coordinating with the local force. What would be ideal, is if we could find some way to get Harris out of the house. If we storm it while she's his hostage, he could kill her."

"What do you know about him that might motivate him to leave?" Hannah asked.

"Possibly a work emergency, but he's turned his phone off. There's no way to reach him."

"Maybe there's a landline at the house. Is there some

way that you could persuade his brother to call him and fabricate an emergency?"

"Roger looked like he was at death's door. He's serving as his brother's guinea pig, testing some new immune therapy drug. He's covered in a rash, barely able to breathe, and looks all jaundiced. I doubt that brotherly compassion would bring Blake running to his side."

"You're describing a serious auto-immune reaction. The brother actually could be at death's door. Who's his oncologist?"

"A guy named Frank Sanderson. Do you know him?"

"I know him well. He's one of Jonathan's partners. Daniel, that's the answer. Blake Harris may not care about his brother, but I'll bet you he cares about his new drug. When you get to Newport Beach, have Frank Sanderson call the landline, tell him the drug is failing, and demand Blake's help with his brother. His blockbuster drug tanking should make him come running."

Hannah hung up the phone and logged into her computer. She pulled up Google Maps and looked for Sandstone Drive. It was a small cul-de-sac ending on the beach. It shouldn't be difficult to find Daniel's team. Hannah didn't ask him if she could be there because she wasn't going to take no for an answer. Andrea was going to need emotional support and possibly medical care when they found her. Grabbing a pack with her first aid kit and her car keys, Hannah headed for the garage.

CHAPTER FIFTY-TWO

W HEN THEY RETURNED TO THE HOUSE, Andrea's jeans were still damp from the ocean and she was chilly.

"If you don't mind, Blake, I'm going to run upstairs and change into some dry clothes. I'm cold."

"Why don't you put on one of those bathing suits I provided? If you're cold, you can warm up in the hot tub. I'll join you." He gave her a smile that made her stomach clench with apprehension. Without answering him, she ran up the stairs.

Blake had only provided one new pair of jeans, but the ones she'd been wearing when he had kidnapped her were in the closet. She grabbed them, along with a fresh pair of socks, and locked herself in the bathroom. After changing, she brushed back the strands of hair that the wind had blown out of the pony tail she'd fashioned that morning. She twisted her hair up and fastened it with a few bobby pins. No makeup. She didn't want to do anything to make herself attractive.

When she stepped out of the bathroom, Blake was

sitting on one of the armchairs in her room. He was wearing a pair of black swim trunks and nothing else. The look on his face chilled her.

"I thought I told you to put on a bikini," he said, raking her body from top to bottom with a glance.

"It's too cold for a bikini. Can't we go down to the patio and have a cup of hot tea and a snack first? I'm hungry after that long walk."

For a moment, she thought he'd agree. But when he got up and walked toward her, one glance confirmed her fear. His arousal was obvious under the thin swim suit. One hand was behind him. She backed away but he grabbed her wrists, spun her around, and immobilized her arms with a pair of handcuffs. She bent forward and kicked his shin as hard as she could. He let go of her.

"I love it when women get feisty and fight back." He grinned at her, rubbing the red mark on his lower leg. "It makes taming them so much more challenging."

"Is this your idea of how to inspire me to leave my family for you?" Andrea asked.

"By the time we're done here, you will want nothing more than to please me, and if leaving your inadequate husband pleases me, you will do it in a heartbeat."

She was about to retort, but realized that was what he wanted. It would turn him on. She gritted her teeth and said nothing. If she was completely passive, maybe he'd get bored.

Blake grabbed her upper arms and pushed her down onto the bed, turning her so he could reach the handcuffs. She heard the scrape of a key, and for a moment thought he was releasing her, but it was only to attach one hand to the brass headboard of the bed. He slipped a cuff on her other wrist and fastened it as well. Then he sat down beside her, gripping her face in his hands and running his fingers along her scalp.

He pulled at her hair until the pins came out, and he draped the long, honey-colored cascade over her shoulders.

"I always thought you looked so sexy with that hair," he said, as he caressed it.

She said nothing.

He got up and walked across the room, and it was then that she noticed he'd brought a sports bag with him. That must be where he'd kept the handcuffs. Reaching in, he removed something, and turned toward her again. He was carrying a large, sharp pair of scissors.

For a moment, she thought he was going to cut her hair off, but he had something else in mind. Unzipping her sweatshirt, he cut his way through her T-shirt and between the cups of her bra, releasing her breasts.

He put both hands on her with a satisfied smile and began to suck at one of her nipples. It hurt and she bit back a grimace. If she couldn't fight him, she wouldn't give him the satisfaction of knowing he'd caused pain.

After a while, with no response from her, Blake pulled back. Then he unzipped her jeans and began to pull them down. Andrea pulled back her legs and kicked at him. Even if her struggles aroused him, she couldn't let him rape her without a fight. Waves of panic, and déjà vu, went through her mind as she held back sobs.

He let go of her, giving her a hard stare.

"That's better. I didn't think you'd give in so easily."

"Blake," she said, in her best therapist tone, "do you really think that raping me is the best way to accomplish your long term goal? If you want a woman to care about you, it's counterproductive."

"I'm not raping you. I'm introducing you to an exciting new sexual experience," he said.

"Exciting for you, maybe. It isn't doing much for me."

Blake broke out in a laugh. "You really are something."

He stood up and took off his swim trunks, letting her see his erection.

"Don't play therapist with me, Andrea. I want you, and nothing is going to prevent me from having you."

CHAPTER FIFTY-THREE

Daniel's team, in unmarked cars, met with the Newport Beach police two blocks from the Harris home. Daniel briefed everyone.

"I've made arrangements with a physician who is taking care of Blake Harris's brother to call him when we're in position and get him to Memorial Hospital. There's a landline at the house. We just don't know if Blake will answer it. Assuming he does, as soon as his car leaves, I want one of our cars to follow him, and I'll arrange to have him met at Memorial by LAPD, where he'll be arrested."

"And if he doesn't leave?" the Newport Beach cop asked.

Brenda pulled out a pile of papers. "We have the architectural plans for the house and we've contacted the security company so we know how to disable the alarm. We'll break in quietly, by the back door to the kitchen, and try to grab Blake before he has an opportunity to hurt Andrea."

Daniel instructed the drivers to park at a distance from one another so that they didn't arouse suspicion but could watch the entrance to the cul-de-sac. Then he called Frank Sanderson and told him it was time.

CHAPTER FIFTY-FOUR

SWEATING AND SATED, BLAKE LAY ATOP Andrea's body. She had fought him until he'd overpowered her, and had then gone limp and unresponsive. He'd been unable to extract a sound of pleasure or of pain from her. Her head was turned away from him, her eyes closed, as if she'd gone somewhere else while he raped her. The experience was far less satisfying than he'd imagined. If she didn't improve, he'd have to get rid of her. What a huge disappointment.

As he was lying there, catching his breath, he heard the landline ring in his bedroom next door. Fucking robocallers. He'd forgotten to disconnect his parents' phone. Three minutes later, it rang again. He got up.

"Don't go anywhere," he told Andrea. "I'm just going next door to disable the phone."

There was no response.

When he got to his bedroom, the damn thing was ringing, yet again. He was about to pull the cord when he recognized the number.

"Hello."

"Dr. Harris. It's Dr. Sanderson. Thank God, I've managed

to reach you. I've tried every number your brother could think of."

"Is something wrong?"

"I need you here, as soon as possible. I'm in the Memorial ICU with Roger. He's had a severe auto-immune reaction to your drug. I've started him on steroids, but you know this drug better than anyone. Maybe between the two of us, we can keep him alive and salvage this trial."

Shit. Leave it to Roger to ruin his week. "I'll leave right now and be there in about an hour," Blake said.

He jumped into the shower, just to wash off the scent of sweat and semen, and dressed quickly. Then, he went back into Andrea's room.

"I have to leave for a few hours." He unfastened the handcuffs. No point in having her pee on the expensive mattress. "Don't worry. I'll be back."

She didn't open her eyes or respond in any way, just lay there. If he hadn't seen her chest rise and fall, he would have wondered if she was dead. Shrugging his shoulders, he left the room and locked it from the outside.

Once in the garage, he fired up his red Maserati. The police would be looking for the black van. The garage door opened and he pressed on the accelerator, speeding out of the cul-de-sac, and heading to the 405 freeway.

CHAPTER FIFTY-FIVE

Daniel's cell rang. It was Sanderson.

"I finally reached him. He's on his way. He said he'd be at Memorial in about an hour."

"Perfect. Thank you for your help," Daniel said.

Daniel hung up and watched until a red sports car emerged and drove away. An unmarked police car followed at a discrete distance. He looked over at Brenda. "Let's go get Andrea."

He was praying she was still alive and not badly hurt. He'd never forgive himself if his timing was wrong.

As they stepped out of their unmarked car, Daniel saw a station wagon headed for the cul-de-sac. It was Hannah's car. He waved at her and she pulled up.

"What are you doing here?"

"Waiting for you to rescue Andrea, so I can take care of her, and don't tell me to go home."

"I wouldn't dream of it," Daniel said. "Your suggestion worked. Blake Harris just left. We're going in to get Andrea."

"I'll come with you."

Daniel shook his head. What if Andrea were dead? He couldn't have Hannah there.

"This is a police operation, Hannah. Please, wait here in your car. I'll call you when we're ready to bring Andrea out. There's crime scene evidence, and police procedure. A civilian involved could sabotage our court case against Harris."

He hoped his argument would be persuasive.

Hannah sighed and got into her car. "Promise me, the instant you find her, you'll call me."

"I promise."

He nodded at Brenda and the two of them jogged down the cul-de-sac to the house.

CHAPTER FIFTY-SIX

ANDREA HEARD THE DOOR CLOSE AS BLAKE LEFT the bedroom. She waited until she could no longer hear his footsteps in the hall. Every muscle in her body ached. Her breasts felt bruised and the severe pain between her legs infuriated her. When she reached down to touch herself, her fingers were wet with blood.

She stumbled to the bathroom, fighting her tears, and the feeling of helplessness that consumed her. She wet a washcloth with cold water and soap, scrubbing her face, her underarms and her chest, wiping his scent from her nostrils. She left the blood on her thighs, which had dried, and put on clean underwear. Last time, she had let her rapist get away with it. This time, she swore it would be different. She was going to get out of here and make sure the son-of-a-bitch paid for this. The rage energized her.

She dressed in her own jeans and the shirt she'd worn to the gym. The thought of putting on anything Blake had bought her made her sick. She found a spare blanket in the closet, and took it to keep warm. It was then that she noticed the sports bag on the floor. Blake had forgotten it.

She unzipped it and removed its contents. The hand-cuffs were still attached to the headboard, but the bag contained a variety of ropes and ties, a large dildo, a whip, and the scissors he'd used to cut off her clothes. She touched the tips and blade and found them to be sharp. At least now, she wasn't defenseless.

Andrea repacked the bag, pushed it under the bed, and placed herself behind the door. She'd only have a moment when he walked in, but she would use that moment well. She was going to stab the fucker as many times as she could. He'd drawn her blood and she was going to reciprocate. She sat there, alert, listening for the sound of the key in the lock.

CHAPTER FIFTY-SEVEN

Daniel and Brenda reached the end of the cul-de-sac. Both of them were armed, although they expected to find the house empty. Avoiding the security cameras, they disabled the alarm, broke a glass pane on the kitchen door, and let themselves in. The kitchen was empty. Working quickly, they explored the ground floor and cleared all the rooms. Daniel motioned to Brenda to follow him upstairs.

A set of double doors at one end of the corridor led to a massive and empty master suite. The bed was neatly made and the bathroom pristine. Clearly, no one was using it. The room next door was a very masculine study: dark wood and leather, and the scent of cigar smoke. The third bedroom had a messy queen-sized bed and male clothing scattered over the floor. A pair of swim trunks lay on the bed, and a laptop occupied a round table near the window.

"Blake's room?" Brenda suggested.

"Probably. There's only one more room on this floor. If she isn't there, we'll check for a cellar."

"Could he have taken her with him, in the back seat or the trunk?"

"Let's hope not."

Daniel tried the handle of the final room and found it locked. Brenda brought out a set of lock picks and began working with them.

Daniel knocked loudly on the door. "Andrea, are you there? Let us in."

There was no answer.

Andrea awoke to the sound of a male voice and someone pounding on the door. There was a scratching sound at the keyhole. A sense of panic came over her. How could she have drifted off when she was trying so hard to stay alert? She jumped to her feet, tossed away the blanket, and gripped the scissors with both hands, ready to respond the instant the door opened.

The final click told Daniel that Brenda had succeeded with her lock picks.

She glanced at him. "After you."

Daniel turned the door handle and opened it wide. The room seemed empty, despite a messy bed with traces of blood he could see from the entryway.

"Andrea, are you in here?" Daniel took a step inside and heard a sound behind him.

Andrea, her eyes wild, ran at him, holding a large pair of scissors in both hands. His martial arts training kicked in automatically, and he disarmed her. She began to scream.

"Andrea, it's Daniel. You're safe. We're getting you out of here."

He held onto her upper arms, trying to get her to look at him.

Finally, she blinked and stared. "Daniel?"

"Yes, Daniel. I've got a whole SWAT team outside to rescue you. You remember Brenda, my partner."

"Where's Blake?"

"He's on his way to LA Memorial Hospital. I've got two guys following him, and two more waiting for him in the ICU, where he'll be arrested for kidnapping."

A look of relief passed over her face.

"Are you hurt?" Daniel asked.

"Where's Jonathan?"

"He's at home with Molly, having a nervous breakdown, waiting for my call. Let's get you out of this house and we can phone him."

She followed him out of the room and down the stairs.

"Brenda, go tell Hannah that Andrea's okay," Daniel said.

"Hannah's here?" Andrea asked.

"I couldn't keep her away. She brought her first aid kit and insisted on being here for you."

A small smile appeared on Andrea's face. "I should have known."

Hannah saw Daniel and Andrea leaving the house and ran to meet them. Andrea's hair was wild, her face tear-stained and her expression dead.

"Sweetheart, I'm so relieved that you're safe." Hannah threw her arms around her friend and Andrea collapsed into them, crying.

"Hannah, take Andrea to your car. We're expecting an

ambulance in a few minutes," Daniel said. "You can go with her to the hospital."

"No hospital," Andrea said. "Hannah's my doctor. I don't want anyone else to touch me."

Hannah looked at her husband. "I've got this."

Putting her arm around Andrea, she led her to the back seat of the station wagon, and joined her there. Taking both of Andrea's hands in hers, she said, "Tell me what happened."

Andrea closed her eyes and turned her head away.

"I was raped," she whispered. "I fought, but he handcuffed me to the bed, and he was stronger."

Hannah squeezed the hands tightly. "I'm so sorry."

"I didn't shower. I know the police need evidence. I just don't want some stranger collecting a rape kit."

"That's why I'm here," Hannah said, "to take care of you. Where else does it hurt?"

"Just sore muscles and probably some bruises. Nothing a hot shower won't help. I need to clean up before I go home. I can't let Jonathan and Molly see me like this."

"We'll go to my house as soon as we can."

"Hannah, what if I get pregnant?"

"I thought you were taking birth control pills."

"I was. I stopped, because we wanted to try for another child. I'm mid-cycle."

"I can give you a morning after pill," Hannah said, "and antibiotics. We'll test for everything and make sure you're safe."

"But what if the pill prevents me from conceiving Jonathan's child?"

"Did it take you a long time to become pregnant with Molly?"

"First try."

"Then don't worry. You need time to heal, physically and

emotionally, before undertaking a pregnancy," Hannah said. "Don't try to deal with this alone. You have people who love you, and you're smart enough to know that some situations require professional help."

"Are you telling the psychiatrist she needs a therapist?" Andrea asked.

"I guess I am."

~

An ambulance arrived a few minutes later, and after Daniel talked to the paramedics, they vacated it so that Hannah could do an examination and obtain evidence with a rape kit, under Brenda's careful supervision. Brenda photographed the bruises on Andrea's wrists, breasts and thighs for evidence. Hannah made an effort to maintain a calm façade, and not show her fury.

When the examination was over, Daniel suggested that Hannah take Andrea home.

"You can come into the station tomorrow and give your statement," Daniel said. "I'm happy to pick you up, if you like."

"I'd better talk to Jonathan," Andrea said. "And tell him I'm going to your house first, so I don't scare Molly when I get home."

Hannah handed her a phone.

Fortunately, it was Christmas week, or the traffic heading north on the 405, in the late afternoon, would have been intolerable. As it was, they got to Hannah and Daniel's house in only an hour.

Hannah gave Andrea a robe, a new bar of soap, a bottle of shampoo, and guided her into the master bathroom. She hoped a hot shower might help to remove the numb look from Andrea's face.

"I'll find some clothes for you to change into. They'll be too big, but at least they'll be comfortable."

Half an hour later, Andrea emerged in a pair of black tights and an oversized cream-colored sweater. Her long hair was damp and twisted into a bun. She had borrowed some blush and lipstick from Hannah's makeup supply and was looking almost normal.

"You know," Hannah said, "when my post-operative patients put lipstick on, I know they're ready to be discharged. We call it the positive lipstick sign."

Andrea gave her a half smile. "Don't read too much into it. You're right about how long it's going to take me to recover from this."

"I know it's going to be difficult," Hannah said. "But I'll be there to help you, I promise, every step of the way."

"By the way," Andrea said, "you might be interested in knowing we may have solved a murder. Blake told me he remembered seeing Roger and his friends gang rape and drown a woman in the family pool. They wrapped up her body and took it away in Roger's car. Blake speculated that they dumped it into the ocean from his father's yacht."

"Do you think he told you the truth?" Hannah asked.

"I do. The dreams he had are all totally consistent with his story, and frankly, after the kidnapping and rape, I think I'm entitled to break patient confidentiality. Tell Daniel, will you?"

"I'll call him."

"Speaking of home, I'm ready to leave. Thank you both for getting me out of there." She threw her arms around Hannah. "You're the best."

CHAPTER FIFTY-EIGHT

BOUT AN HOUR AFTER HANNAH HAD DRIVEN away, Daniel got a call from his team.

"We've arrested him, booked him, and he's cooling his heels in a cell at the station, waiting for you to question him. He's already called his hot shot lawyer."

"Fine. Let him stew. I'll question him tomorrow. The forensic team is going over this house as we speak, and I'll be getting a statement from Dr. Marcus tomorrow as well. We've got enough evidence to put him away for a very long time."

An hour later, he got a call from Hannah. Daniel listened to the details and shared them with Brenda.

"You know," Brenda said, "sometimes I just can't understand how someone as smart and rich and successful as Blake Harris can fuck up his life so badly. What makes him tick?"

Daniel shrugged. "Something in his early life must have made him the psychopath he became."

"I'm so glad this story has a happy ending. Andrea could have ended up dead. We don't always get there in time."

"I wouldn't call it a happy ending," Daniel said. "But at least it isn't a tragic one. I'm not sure Hannah would ever have forgiven me, if we hadn't been able to bring Andrea home."

"Is it possible to prosecute Roger and his friends? I know there wasn't any forensic evidence, and I doubt the testimony of Blake Harris would be useful. He was just a kid at the time, and a defense attorney would rip his testimony to pieces," Brenda said.

"The only way to get Blake to testify against Roger would be to cut a deal with him for a more lenient sentence for rape and kidnapping. I wouldn't even suggest it to the prosecutor. I want to see that bastard in prison for a very long time."

"What about Roger?" Brenda asked. "He's at the end of his life. Maybe you could get him to confess to clear his conscience, and identify his friends."

"That's a good thought. Although I doubt he'll live long enough to be tried for murder."

"You can never predict when someone will die. If they charge him, and his friends, maybe you could do a video deposition, just in case he dies before trial."

"Not a bad idea," Daniel said. "We could also send a forensic team to check out the Harris yacht for trace evidence. After I interrogate Blake tomorrow morning, I'll have a talk with the prosecutor and see what she thinks. The important thing is, we found Andrea."

CHAPTER FIFTY-NINE

"MOMMY, I MISSED YOU. WHERE WERE YOU?" Molly came running into the hall as soon as Andrea opened the door.

Andrea bent down and picked her up, hugging her tightly.

"I missed you too, sweetie. Did you have a fun sleepover?"

Molly's hair smelled of baby shampoo and her skin was like silk. Andrea buried her nose in Molly's neck, fighting back tears at the thought she might have died and never gotten to hold her child again.

"We baked chocolate chip cookies and watched cartoons," Molly said. "I brought some home for you."

"Thank goodness. I'm starving," Andrea said. "Lead the way."

Jonathan waited for Molly to run into the kitchen before he took Andrea into his arms. She stiffened.

"Don't," she said. "I'll start to cry in front of Molly. Wait until she's asleep and I'll tell you everything. What took you so long to find me?"

"Believe me, Daniel had practically the whole Westside station, working twenty-four hour shifts, trying to figure out where he'd taken you, and how to get you out safely. I was so scared." There were tears in his eyes.

She squeezed his hand. "Come feed me. What I need right now is a big dose of you and Molly."

"And chocolate chip cookies?"

"Definitely cookies, and a large cup of very strong coffee."

It was late, and Andrea was exhausted by the time Molly was finally persuaded to go to bed. She tucked Molly in, and joined Jonathan in the master bedroom.

He put his arms around her and she finally allowed herself to collapse against his chest and cry. He held her until she was out of tears.

"Do you want to talk about it, or are you too tired?"

"I'm tired, but I'm also agitated. I don't think I'll be able to fall asleep until I tell you everything."

Could she tell him everything? Would he see her differently afterwards? As a victim? A liar? Someone he didn't want to be married to any longer?

Jonathan led her to a comfortable armchair and sat down, drawing her towards his lap.

She pulled away. "I can't sit."

He let her go and she paced the bedroom, her breathing growing faster and more agitated.

"Tell me, sweetheart," he said.

"He grabbed me in the parking lot and shot me up with Ketamine. I didn't come out of it for five hours and I had horrible hallucinations. He apologized and told me he intended to give me a wonderful, relaxing vacation week, and to persuade me to leave you for him. He promised me the best sex of my life, and gave me bags of designer clothes and diamonds from Tiffany's."

She continued, still pacing, but watching his face.

"He was polite and charming the whole first day, and the next morning, he took me for a walk on the beach. We were at his parent's home, in a wealthy enclave where the beach is almost private."

"Daniel had cops watching all his homes. We didn't know where you were, but fortunately, you were seen on the beach. As soon as they had confirmation, Daniel got a team together to rescue you," Jonathan said.

New tears began to fall down Andrea's cheeks. "I knew you and Daniel and Hannah would find me. I just had to hold him off until you did. Unfortunately, I wasn't successful."

"Did he hurt you, darling?"

She turned away from him, so he couldn't see her face.

"He came to my room, handcuffed me to the bed and raped me. He's into S&M. I knew that from his therapy and I was so scared. I feel filthy."

Jonathan got up, walked over, turned her to face him, and cupped her face in his hands. "He's the filthy one. You're not to blame for any of this."

"I fought him, Jonathan, as hard as I could, but he was much stronger, and my hands were cuffed. All I could do was kick."

"Darling, I'm just glad you're alive. You can't imagine the nightmares I had about losing you. I know you did the best you could to fight him. None of this is your fault, and he's going to jail for a very long time."

"I'm going to help put him there, Jonathan. I gave a rape

sample and I'm going to testify. This time, I won't let a rapist get away with it."

"This time?" He gave her a quizzical look.

She drew away, so she could see his face. She hadn't yet decided if she was going to tell him about the first time, but she'd slipped up. Now, she had to.

"I never told you. I was raped in college; Freshman year, at a fraternity party. I was still a virgin when it happened, and I was so ashamed, I couldn't tell anyone. The guy who did it is probably still out there, having the time of his life."

"Why didn't you tell me?" Jonathan asked. "Did you think you couldn't trust me with the biggest trauma of your life? I thought we had no secrets from one another."

"I thought I'd put it behind me. I didn't want to dredge it up again, and I didn't know how you would feel about me if you knew."

Jonathan raised his eyebrows. "Were you truly afraid that I'd love you less if I knew you'd had a horrific experience?"

"I didn't know."

She still didn't know. He could be loving to her now, but what about later, once he had time to process all this? Would he ever fully trust her again?

"Let's set it to rest then. You can always count on me to be there for you, no matter what. I'm going to help you in any way I can to get through this. We're a team. Blake Harris didn't just rape you. He attacked our marriage, and we're going to make sure he doesn't have the opportunity to hurt anyone else, ever again."

Andrea collapsed back onto his chest and he held her tight. Her breathing became deep and regular. He took her to their bed, and tucked her in.

She closed her eyes and tried to sleep, but she was still too agitated. She felt Jonathan climbing into bed next to her.

His hands caressed her hair and he kissed her forehead. Then he wrapped his body around hers and held her. She breathed more deeply and let herself relax into his arms. Maybe she could cope, after all. Finally, she allowed herself to fall asleep.

CHAPTER SIXTY

I T WAS AFTER MIDNIGHT. HANNAH HAD WAITED for Daniel to come home. He looked exhausted. Sitting down on the bed, he reached over and kissed her forehead.

"Thanks for waiting up. How's Andrea doing?"

"She's pretty traumatized, but she's tough. We'll all help her get through this. She has a wonderful husband who adores her, and I know Jonathan will do everything possible."

Daniel took her hands in his. "You have one of those too, you know, a husband who adores you."

Hannah smiled. "I know. I can't thank you enough for all you did to find Andrea. I think I would have completely decompensated if she'd been killed, but I trusted you to do everything humanly possible, and you did."

"Does that mean you forgive me for the honeymoon from hell?"

"It means we're a great team, and who wants to break that up?"

She opened her arms to him and he held her close. She

heard his breathing quicken and felt his hands caressing her back and shoulders. Pulling back, she looked at the love on his face, and leaned in for a kiss.

ACKNOWLEDGMENTS

As always, many people contributed to this manuscript. First and foremost, I thank my wonderful developmental editor, Linda Schreyer, for her insightful feedback. My publisher, Christiana Miller of Third Street Press took care of the formatting, the copy editing and the marketing. Kristin Bryant designed the cover.

Two close friends, Dr. F. David Rudnick and Dr. Sheri Fried, were my sources for all things psychiatric. Mark Sherwood introduced me to the world of start-ups, and Senior Lead Officer Maria Gray of the LAPD answered my police procedural questions. My writer's retreat group, Darlene, Erica, Cathy, Hyla and Laurie gave their usual constructive criticism. Finally, I thank my husband Uri, who has always been my first reader.

ABOUT THE AUTHOR

PAULA BERNSTEIN is a New York native, who migrated to LA to attend graduate school in Chemistry. She acquired a PhD, an exceptionally nice husband, and the ability to synthesize creative meals from leftovers. Not long afterwards, she escaped her laboratory and attended medical school.

Like her series heroine, Hannah Kline, Paula spent her professional life practicing Obstetrics and Gynecology. When she developed an irresistible desire for an uninterrupted nights' sleep, she retired from her full time practice, and reinvented herself as a writer of medical mysteries.

Learn more about her at her website:
www.hannahklinemysteries.com

The Hannah Kline Mysteries

Murder in the Family

Murder by Lethal Injection

Murder in a Private School

Murder in the Goldilocks Zone

Murder in Vitro

Murder on Her Honeymoon

Murder is a Nightmare

Murder is a Hate Crime

Murder is Paralyzing

Short Stories

Potpourri

www.ingramcontent.com/pod-product-compliance
Lightning Source LLC
Chambersburg PA
CBHW021429150726
47989CB00001B/170